EXOGENY

Nathan Karl

Copyright © 2022 Nathan Karl
NathanKarlBooks@gmail.com

All rights reserved.

ISBN 978-1-0880-5771-1

No part of this book may be reproduced or used in any manner without the prior written permission of the copyright owner, except for the use of brief quotations in a book review.

Edited by Jason Green
theartsstl.com

Cover art by Patrick Weck
patrickweck.artstation.com

For my Josie.

Exogeny

Beth was an orphan. A rogue planet with no sun or star to call her own. Her delicate orbit decayed, ejecting her from a faraway solar system. For eons, she drifted across silent space, cold and dead. Finally, she happened upon a friend. A meteor just as lost and lonely as she. Their chance encounter, a violent meeting between bodies, left her with a deep scar. She was not bothered by the blemish, just happy for the company. The surviving scraps of meteor and crust spent long uncounted cycles reeling from the collision in a tight revolution above her face. In time, the debris condensed into a primordial moon called Intiloch. It was a small moon, but it dominated her sky. Unsettled plates erupted out of seas of magma. Swirling waves of embers fought to take shape around an unformed core. The surface constantly changed as new concretions darkened, only to be washed under the lava and dissolved in the heat. Intiloch's chaos warmed Beth's surface with a scarlet glow. Soon, relative to her cosmic scale, more friends appeared.

Neta took slow, deliberate steps through the canyon's black sand. She did not consider herself a friend, especially not to the planet below her—a reluctant acquaintance at best. The flashlight on her wristband illuminated a trail of bootprints, growing forgotten in the slightest breeze. She followed them through a village of beehive-shaped huts woven of dried tawny reeds, erected around and between the geodesic domes of Colony2. The trail led her up the side of a dune, each step loosening and pushing down sand.

"That took you too long," a voice said over the shortwave radio clipped to her belt and connected to a headset by a thin wire. It belonged to the man at the top of the dune. Commander Erickson was dressed identically to Neta in a light-blue jumpsuit adorned with a round glass helmet and wheezing air filtration system. A blaster rifle pressed against his shoulder.

"I needed a tape-up," said Neta, out of breath from the hike. She stopped beside him on the crest and lifted her arm to show a new length of fabric patching along the side. He didn't look. "It's going to be more tape than anything soon," she added, refusing to apologize.

"Hmm," the commanding officer said, scanning the opposite side of the dune. The red rays of Intiloch bloomed like an iris peeking over the canyon wall. His rifle tracked a green leafy plant racing across the black sands.

"But why should it be any different than the rest of the colony," Neta added and took a deep inhale of filtered air. Her mouth filled with crisp static electricity. Each breath from the helmet reminded her of rubbing her hair in a wool blanket as a child. A long sip of lukewarm coffee from her hydration pack washed away the flavor. You don't travel to the other side of the galaxy to be reminded of home. It was her second day of reusing the same ground beans. She could probably stretch them out another day to conserve her ration. The dissipating caffeine had so far done nothing to alleviate her near-chronic exhaustion or the swollen bags under her eyes, almond-shaped and colored, on her round face. It had been years since she slept well, though she had only arrived on Beth a little over a month past.

"I'd say your suit is holding up better than the colony, actually," he said, pointing to a thin pillar of smoke rising behind them. "The communication center is going to need more than tape. You should probably find a new desk." In the night, a sandstorm uprooted the radio tower. A group of Colony2's more expendable crew members worked to put out the remaining fire from where the antenna had speared through the flimsy plastic walls of the communication center.

Erickson's blaster lit up the dark dawn with a beam of bright blue plasma racing over the desert floor. The bush tumbled over, expelling a mist of fine powder before the energized snap of the rifle's report could sound.

"You shot a tumbleweed?" Neta asked.

"Under that mess of leaves is a shrubrat," Erickson said. "Those spores it shits out when it dies can clog up the filters real bad. It's better to take care of it before it gets too close to the colony."

Neta frowned. It was the reason she had avoided exiting the safety of the airlocks. The air within Beth's canyon was perfectly breathable. Planets like it were surprisingly easy to find. The microbes, bacteria, and viruses, the things that couldn't be seen, all unique to each new planet and deadly to the visiting colonists:

those were the difficult parts of colonization.

"It looks like they're ready for us," Neta said. A crewmember waved them down from the remains of the burnt-out dome. Erickson took a last admiring glance at his kill. He slung the rifle over his shoulder, trying not to look too smug. He took great pride in his accuracy.

"All things considered, she lasted longer than she was supposed to," Neta said, careful to follow the commander down the dune. "And outlived all of Colony3 by a few months."

"That's not reassuring."

"These domes were only supposed to last a couple years, right?"

"That's right," Erickson said uneasily.

"How long has it been since you passed those couple years?" Neta asked.

He said nothing, only grunted in confirmation.

"This mean we'll get pulled?" the waving laborer asked over the shortwave as they came into range, his fishbowl helmet clouded as he struggled to lift the end of a server rack slick with fire suppression foam.

"Doubtful," Erickson replied, stepping through a large hole melted in the cheap white frame of Colony2's former communication center. "We've been in worse situations. The lawyers didn't find evacuation necessary then."

"After Colony3 went belly-up, you said if anything else happened, they'd get us off of here, right?" the laborer asked.

"Right," Neta agreed. She stepped up to the charred black and bubbled foundation but did not cross over.

"But what do we need to do," she asked rhetorically, "to let those lawyers know that our communications are down?"

The laborer shrugged. His wet eyes sank further into their sockets as he pondered the situation. The crewman on the other end laid down his side of the server, growing impatient for his partner to start moving.

"We'll need to get the tower working again, which means we won't have a problem worth pulling us for," she explained, pulling from the several weeks of correspondence courses she had received en route to the planet, the only qualifications she had as Colony2's Communication Officer. Terraforming work was undesirable and high-risk, a combination that often led to subpar hiring practices. The pay was good and, if not for low standards, Neta wouldn't have a job. "It's doable, but it'll take a couple of days," she added.

"We need to find out if anything is salvageable," said Erickson, pulling a monitor out of the thick carpeting of foam. He squinted into the pale swirl of the degaussed display and carried it over to Neta.

"Wristband, download the system data," Neta said to her device, commanding it to begin the task. Nothing happened. She sighed and clicked a few buttons, beginning the process manually.

"These models don't do complex tasks on voice command. You're lucky if it'll turn on the flashlight or go on mute," Erickson told her. "No expense spared by the Cornflower Mining Company."

Shortly after her arrival—only hours, really—the Cornflower Mining Company filed for bankruptcy, a casualty of too many intergalactic corporate battles. Their assets were to be divided by a legal moderator and auctioned to the highest bidders. This arrangement left the short-term settlements in a limbo of red tape and dilapidating shelters. The planet's three colonies, now two, were ordered to cease all operations. The massive World Builders—responsible for terraforming the canyon—were deactivated remotely. On clear nights, a stalled supply ship teased the workers with permanent shelters, food, and equipment they would likely never see. Potentially, the supplies could be auctioned off separate from the planet below. The needs of Cornflower's creditors were to be taken into account before those of the workers.

"Whatever wasn't crushed by the tower was burnt up in the fire," she said, scrolling through her wristband's small screen. "If anything survived that, the water and extinguishers probably finished the job."

The distorted text of the cracked, round screen illuminated the whiskers across Erickson's jaw. There was no reason he shouldn't have been commanding a transport ship or exploratory crew, Neta thought. Commanding a terraforming crew seemed a waste of his potential. He was a capable leader. And even though it shouldn't carry as much weight—though it often did—he was handsome enough.

"Did we have any word from Colony1 before the storm hit?" Erickson asked.

"Nothing from Colony1," she said.

"What about the backups?" he asked, setting the monitor back into the mess at his feet.

"The backups are fried."

"Check the shortrange radios," he told her. "If they route directly through the generators, they could boost enough to get some kind of signal through."

Neta frowned doubtfully. Colony1 was too far away for the shortrange. Too many obstacles across the valley and electrical interference from the smoldering moon blocked the signal.

"Just do it," he commanded, standing tall among the crew. "Ordering, not asking. Colony1 was dead center of the storm last night. We were only on the outskirts. I don't think we could have survived a harder hit than what we got."

Neta shook her head. "No distress calls, signals, or messages. Nothing from Colony1. We can't really know until the tower is back up." Aside from the loss of life, the morale of Colony2 couldn't handle the cosmic loneliness if their only remaining sister settlement was gone.

"I'll get some of the natives on it when they wake," Erickson said, looking past the blackened remains of the ruined dome to the moon moving along its path above the canyon walls. The planet's dominant native species, simply named Bethians, were enslaved to their circadian rhythms. The moment the burning moon set over the horizon, the natives slept until it rose again. It didn't matter where the Bethians were or what they were doing. They were beholden to their sleep.

"What's that?" Erickson asked, moving his focus to a pinprick dropping from the firmament, a white cylindrical rocket, cone-tipped with four red-colored fins placed around its circumference, reflecting in the maroon light. "Is that a StarHopper?"

"They're cutting it real close," Neta said. The StarHopper was the type of ship that demanded attention, the new and shiny toy of a trust fund kid who wanted you to know that he knows he's better than you. She had known kids like that once. They had left her with a broken nose that had not healed properly and taken two of her molars. It was a stark contrast from the utilitarian cruisers that visited backwater planets, like the bulky and utilitarian mass-transport that hung in Beth's orbit.

"You didn't know we had an arrival?"

"Nope." She sipped her cold coffee and motioned to the downed tower.

"Shit, they never got the landing protocols?"

Two things made life possible within Beth's canyon: first, the warmth of the smoldering moon; and second, a blanket of breathable atmosphere. Intiloch's orbit lay so close to the planet's surface that any ill-prepared ship trying to pass during the day would find itself consumed by intense heat. And so sudden was the atmosphere, held in place by the canyon walls, that entering at speeds above sub-sonic would be akin to flying into a brick wall. Safe descent to the surface was only possible if taken slowly in the empty night sky. It was Neta's job to communicate this information. She hadn't had the chance. But the StarHopper wasn't coming in slowly, it was in a last-minute push to put as much distance between it and the burning moon as possible, the pilot flying like a new ship could easily be bought when the chrome latch handles began to tarnish.

Exogeny

"The last thing we need is a group of tourists turning their ship into a pressure cooker," Erickson said. A cheaper ship would have collapsed in on itself. The StarHopper jostled as it reached each new thin layer of gas, but it held together—the miracles of deep pockets. A set of side thrusters sparked for only an instant, spinning the ship around and pointing the rocket's igniting engines planetside. Blue flames erupted downward to slow the descent. Erickson sighed with an angry relief.

"Will you go find Agda?" Erickson asked, "she'll have the paperwork visitors need to sign. Releases and stuff. It's usually better if she isn't alone during the meet and greets. Not everyone is—" he paused to consider the best phrasing, eyeing the company-issued blaster pistol at Neta's hip, "—as accepting."

"Agda?" Neta asked, finding a short armadillo-like Bethian sitting upright at the thatched entrance of a beehive-shaped hut. Sleepy excitement dazzled from small button eyes, staring out into the red daylight.

"We have visitors," Agda said with sincere excitement in a gravelly voice. Her vocal cords—buried deep within a leathery segmented exoskeleton—hadn't been meant for human language.

"We're supposed to roll out the welcoming committee," Neta told her.

"I watched them land," Agda said dreamily. "I cannot remember the last time I was awake to see a landing. Intiloch is already so high."

"I think you almost watched them die," Neta said. She offered a gloved hand to help Agda to her hooved feet. They walked through the sand to the nearest working airlock, past identical huts of waking Bethians. Another member of the indigenous species stopped them from the entrance of its home. The creature looked exactly the same as Agda, all adult Bethians did. They spoke in a low droning bellow punctuated by the occasional clicking of pincers housed in their throats. Following a quick back and forth, Agda continued with Neta on their way.

"Sorry, about that," Agda apologized.

"It's alright, part of my job is supposed to be trying to understand the language. You each said the Bethian equivalent of your names, and 'Intiloch has risen to protect us.' Is that right?"

"Almost," Agda told her, searching the sand for the words to explain. "Our eyes developed under the smoldering moon, where the light is duller, so visual identification was low on our evolutionary to-do list." She gave a practiced raspy chuckle. "That is why we start each new idea by announcing our names. Proper nouns are as embellished as our language gets. We otherwise communicate emotional feelings to each other. So, what I really said was closer to, 'Agda. Intiloch. Safe.' Everything else is mostly unnecessary."

"Well, you've managed to learn a lot in such a short time," Neta said.

Agda laughed. "It wasn't so hard," she said cheerily. "I think maybe humans like to believe they're a little more advanced than they actually are."

"I hope you're ready to put that theory to the test. Guessing by the type of ship they're flying, I'd say our guests might think pretty highly of themselves."

"Will they have any supplies for the colony?" Agda asked. She handed Neta a pair of welder's goggles to shield her eyes from the bright fluorescent lights the settlers used.

"Doubtful. Anyone who provides any aid could be seen as claiming a stake in Cornflower's mineral rights. But they could also be held liable for the colony's well-being," Neta said. She secured the goggles over Agda's eyes. "Probably here to assess the situation. Don't expect any commitments. Especially in our condition."

"New buyers?" Agda asked.

Neta nodded. Two mechanical doors closed behind them and failed. The doors re-opened, tried to close again, and failed. Neta found a series of colorfully lit buttons along the airlock wall. She quickly put a stop to the mechanical chomping.

"Erickson said maybe we could be bought by a conservancy. Is this them?" Agda asked.

"Not with the ship that's landing. The only ones that can afford a StarHopper are in it for the profit. Try not to get your hopes up about it. Even as-is, no conservation group could afford a whole planet. It would need to be donated outright." Neta swiped a layer of sand from the bottom door and hit the control panel again.

"Your people make things very complicated," Agda said as the chamber filled with a sterilizing agent.

"We really do," Neta agreed. A screen on the wall flashed an all-clear message, indicating no traces of outside microbes. She removed her helmet and gloves.

"That is getting worse," Agda said, turning her attention to Neta's arm as she rolled up the sleeves of her jumpsuit to reveal a light-brown smear along the outside of her forearm. It had started the week as an ashy blemish that wouldn't wash away. "I don't think that is just a rash."

"Has it?" Neta asked, she twisted her arm to look at it. "It's gotten hard too. Like a callous."

"You should let Doctor Canalis take a look at it."

"Maybe later," Neta said.

The tourists quickly made their way from the jetway, anxious for solid footing after their turbulent landing. Neta and Agda found them comfortably spread throughout the colony's commissary. They were a stark contrast to the weathered room, clean and well-nourished in unstained white jumpsuits. One of the men sat on a bench at the far end of the long table, flashing a serpentine smirk at the expense of a haggard plumber on the other side. Another stood at the cafeteria line speaking to the cook's daughter, a pale girl that divvied out rations to the crew. Long curly hair rested on the shoulders of his spacesuit, unzipped to display a thick matte of chest hair. The last of the visitors leaned against the wall near the doorway, the decaying veneer peeling away from the frame. He was tall, his arms crossed over his chest, coldly watching the room through a thick pair of glasses.

The first two reminded Neta of "actors" in the films playing in the sleazy theatre below the apartment she spent her childhood in, just a single room they were lucky to share with only one other family. The third tourist looked more like one of the theatre's anonymous patrons, an empty stick figure only moving to chew on a glob of gum.

"How much do you make in a month?" the man at the table asked the plumber, "50? 100 credits? I'll pay that right now for a bottle."

The plumber shook his head silently, staring down into the bowl with hollowed eyes at the only warm meal he'd be rationed for the day. Neta had known hunger before. Real hunger. The type that left her confused and exhausted. Too far gone to feel the pangs of an empty stomach. They weren't there yet, but they were getting close. She stepped forward, leaving Agda standing awkwardly behind.

"Come on now. Don't be greedy. We stopped at a waystation about three systems back. They couldn't stop talking about the hooch made out here in the void." The outsider leaned forward against the table, running a hand through his coiffed hair, dyed a deep black like his mustache. "You know what I'm talking about. The good stuff you'd make in one of those bathtubs. Strong enough to get our ship back off the ground.

"One a' y'all here has to be brewin'," the man said, adding an exaggerated drawl, "and you look like the kind of ol' hound dog who would know where to find it, am I right?"

Neta put her hand on the plumber's thin shoulder. "Hey, Harry. I've got it from here," she reassured him. "I think Erickson needs you to check the well filters. Make sure they're still operating after the fire."

Harry nodded. He pulled himself away from the table, taking his bowl with him. He smelled of earthy dust as he walked past. The plumber had hardly said more than a few words to her unrelated to sanitation. He had been at Colony2 before she had arrived. She assumed he would be here after she left.

"I'm afraid we ran out of hooch months ago," Neta said, eyeing the visitors suspiciously as she took Harry's spot across the table. His scent lingered. Neta was sure she didn't smell much better. "Water is all we can spare as far as provisions and supplies go. Everything else, food, medicine, fuel, all rationed and accounted for." She looked around the room. The tourist made no attempt to hide his amusement.

"Oh, that's quite alright, darlin'. We've got plenty of our own," the man said in his mocking tone. "It doesn't sound like even the water is very trustworthy."

Neta bit her tongue and forced a polite smile. The stranger was right, which bothered her even more. A minor filtration failure now would be another devastation to the colony.

"We should start over. My name's Neta," she said slyly, resting her arm on the table. "We'll need to get some signatures from you. Just the three of you? Let me just pull up the paperwork, really quick."

She pressed a button on her silver wristband. Not-by-accident, the flashlight illuminated directly into the man's eyes. He cursed and quickly turned away. The setting was higher than Neta had intended, but she wasn't sorry for it. "My apologies," she feigned. She tapped several other buttons, skipping over a photo gallery. The moving image of an olive-skinned child taking awkward steps forward quickly disappeared into static on the small screen.

"I'm so sorry about that," she continued, "I'm still pretty new. Haven't quite figured out all the buttons on this thing yet."

"Fine, it's fine," the man with the coiffed hair said, dropping the accent. He rubbed his eyes to push away the blobs of white. "I'm Eddy, over there is Rob, and pouting against the wall is Judge," pointing out his fellow travelers as he spoke.

"Judge or the Judge?" Neta turned and asked. "Is that a name or a title?"

The Judge's eyes frowned at her over his glasses. She wondered if he cared much for his fellow travelers. His poise gave the presence of being much older than the others, though his face, weathered with pockmarks and dark splotches, lacked the lines to define any actual age.

"May I ask what brings you to our little planet?" she asked, turning back.

Eddy blinked hard over to Rob for approval, but he was too distracted by his conversation with the cook's daughter to notice. The Judge cleared his throat and nodded his approval to Eddy—the low man of the team.

"I'm sure you already know. It doesn't look like you get many visitors, even before the bankruptcy. We're here to appraise. Make sure the equipment and planet are really worth the investment."

"You didn't need to come all this way," Neta said, "that data is available with the lawyers."

Eddy leaned forward. "Planets aren't cheap. Especially this one. Atmosphere. Mineral deposits. Everything of value is limited to just this canyon. The rest of the planet is uninhabitable. Too treacherous for long term mining operations. But we can't just buy the canyon. We have to buy the entirety of Beth. We represent a small firm. We need to be careful with the types of investments we take on. Data can be exaggerated or faked. We're doing our due diligence to make sure that it's not."

From across the room, the sound of skin hitting skin interrupted their conversation. The cook's daughter had struck Rob, his chest hair on full display, with an open palm. Upset, she fled through the swinging door that divided the seating from the kitchen. He laughed and started walking towards the rest of his group, parading the red mark on his cheek like a badge of honor. He clapped Eddy on the shoulder, proud of himself for the reaction he had received. "We'll also be doing a bit of sightseeing while we're here," Rob said.

"Sightseeing?" Neta asked, confused. The grey mountains and black sand she had seen so far had left her wanting.

"That's right," Rob said, "take in the views, do a little exploring."

"This planet and its environment are unique: no star, no system, just a hot, bright moon. Life developed on Beth in ways it never has before. When you start terraforming again—whether we buy you or not, it's only a matter of time—you're going to strip away all of what makes this planet unique. An entire ecosystem wiped out. First, the bacteria. Then things that eat the bacteria, the things that eat those things, and up and up. All replaced with trees and grass, and finally the same animals and birds that you can find on any colony," Eddy said.

"Like your ruttlehorns," Rob said, "I'd like to get one for my collection while I still can."

"So, you're not just sightseeing. You're trophy hunting?" Neta asked. Besides the Bethians, there were just a handful of other species on the undeveloped planet. Ruttlehorns were large aggressive beasts crowned by a series of hollow horns, sounding an ominous tone with each breath.

"Only of the lesser species," Eddy said, looking back at Agda, standing still at the doorway, looking very much like a deer caught in the headlights.

The Judge came to life behind them, forcing his way into the conversation. "It wouldn't be the first time, though, would it? The way they're telling it, the Cornflower team found your people asleep, thought you were dumb and docile." He paused to smile as if he was about to deliver a favorite punchline. "They didn't realize they were dealing with an intelligent species until they'd already eaten a few of you."

The bright-blue chewing gum flopped around in his mouth as he talked, stepping closer and closer to the little Bethian. His voice was deep and free of inflection, not offering apologies or condolences. "Did they tell you about all of this, what would happen to your planet, that their terraforming would kill everything first?"

The kitchen door punched open. The bottom

hinges broke with a crash. Mr. Lolo, the cook, a large Slavic man with a greying beard and hair tied back in a ponytail, held a paring knife in one hand as he leaped the length of the room. He clutched Rob's long feathered hair in his free hand. The silliness of Lolo's name betrayed his size. "Do you know how old she is?" he screamed, aware of what Rob had said to his daughter. Before the chef could raise the paring knife to Rob's throat, the Judge was between them, stretching his long frame to complete the trip in just a few strides. He grasped the chef's face in his hand and shoved the heavier man off his feet, slamming him down against the floor.

In an instant, the commissary was pure noise. Agda let out a warbled croak in shock. Eddy and Rob began shouting incoherent curses among themselves. From the broken doorway, Lolo's daughter shrieked. Neta's bench screeched against the floor as she got to her feet.

"Do you have any idea who we are?" The Judge asked with a smile through the back of his hand. His skeletal fingers unwrapped from around Lolo's head like it was nothing more than a child's ball, allowing him to kick with a thick-soled boot. He began delivering heavy blows to the chef's stomach, one after another.

Neta's thoughts turned to finding help. To finding Erickson. She had always preferred flight over fight. The exit was on the opposite side of the dome. The assault lay between. Mr. Lolo spat blood with each successive kick. She sprinted, sure she could get past. She could not. The Judge grabbed her by the arm. He locked his cold eyes on hers, pausing his attack on the Russian. She returned his gaze and found nothing. He was a void vaster than the one the planet sauntered through, and it terrified her. She felt a flash of hate for the fear he commanded over her. His hand tightened around her arm, she felt the bone begin to ache. Pressure built along the inside of the hardened rash. Out of spite, she swallowed the pain, resolved to show no emotion, damned if she would allow her face to betray her. Something cracked in his grip. The white pain of an exposed nerve ran up her arm and through her clavicle, a deep burn stabbed by an ice-cold knife. A sound formed in her throat, she wasn't sure if it ever escaped. He threw her across the room, proving stronger than his thin body suggested. The Judge turned away and knelt over the Russian, pushing a heavy blaster into his chest.

Neta landed on her feet, pulling her raygun from the holster at her waist. Calmly, the Judge took the bright-blue piece of gum out of his mouth, and using his thumb pressed it to Lolo's forehead, forcing it to stick. His trigger finger held steady. Neta couldn't say the same for her own. The pistol rattled in her hand as she pointed it at her assailant. "Why don't we all just take a breath," she requested, aware of the pain in her arm, sharply pulsing to the rhythm of her heartbeat.

"You sure you'll make the shot from there?" the Judge growled. "It'd be a real shame if you missed."

"He's right. It'd rip right through the wall," Rob said. He took a cautious step forward. The Judge quickly met his gaze with a disapproving shake of the head and a grim smirk, stopping him in his tracks. Neta realized she wasn't the only one afraid of him.

"That would contaminate the entire room, probably the entire colony," the Judge said.

That would only happen if she could take a shot. She couldn't. She hadn't bothered to charge the blaster's core since she arrived on Beth last month. The buyers didn't need to know this. They wouldn't find out as long as she never pulled the trigger. Her only hope was to force a stalemate. Eddy, feathered black perm and mustache, was close enough that no one would question if she could miss. Immediately her gun was pointing at the seated man, not expecting to be involved in the standoff.

"Mr. Lolo, you first. Put the knife down," Neta ordered. Eddy nodded in agreement, his eyes crossing down her hollow barrel.

"Now, isn't that better?" she asked, noticing Eddy's gaze quickly shifted to her arm. The light-brown smear had cracked like a thin sheet of balsa wood, split open along the grain. Blood ran in quick drips down a loose hanging splinter.

The walls of the medical dome were a whiter white than any of the others, reminding Neta that the rest of the colony, not nearly as valuable, had begun to yellow. It was the most secure of the structures in the settlement, constructed with a reinforced frame and operating off of an independent air and water filtration system. It would be the only building that remained once terraforming was complete. Neta looked around the room at the strange, polished metal boxes, some topped with glass orbs, others with small doors asking to have samples inserted or tools taken out, all covered in flashing lights and buttons. She was unsure of what any of the equipment did, she only knew that it was important and expensive enough for the company to invest money into protecting it.

The camp's doctor closely inspected her arm, shaking her head, hemming and hawing, before applying a thin bandage. Neta had spent hours undergoing a series of physical scans. It would take some time before the expensive machines returned her results. Neta waited restlessly at the doctor's unused workstation, trying to distract herself with the colony's communication networks, remotely reformatting an array of systems meant to operate the deactivated World Builders. Her focus faltered. She replayed the altercation in her mind, imagining what she would have done differently. If her blaster had been charged, would she have been able to use it?

Through a porthole window, she watched a team of laboring Bethians pour polymer concrete into a square frame. The tower wouldn't be attached to the new base until tomorrow. They would be unable to contact Colony1 for another night, leaving the settlement's fate unknown.

"That one looks like the Alkayon," Agda said from the doorway, pointing up at a swirling dark patch of cooled magma on Intiloch's surface. A game Neta had seen Erickson play with the little Bethian to find recognizable shapes on its surface, like searching for images in the clouds. Neta hadn't seen her since the confrontation, and she wasn't in the mood to be cheered up.

"The what?" she asked, refusing to look. She wanted someone else to be as angry as she was.

"The Alkayon. The spiraling stone tower my ancestors built to reach the moon, have I never told you the stories?" Agda asked, getting excited to share the folktales of her tribe.

"No, but how about another time," Neta said bitterly, her thoughts drifting back to the events in the commissary. "How is Lolo's daughter doing?"

"Upset still. I don't know what he said to her."

"Yeah, I can make a few guesses."

"Erickson sent them on their way," Agda said. At some point during their little stand-off, she had fled for the commander.

"I saw, they headed toward the Stacks in a couple of SRVs," Neta said, referring to a pair of upscale brand ShuttleCrawler Recreation Vehicles, long metallic trapezoids, propelled by eight hydraulic powered mechanical legs ending in trifurcated pads to grip and climb over the toughest terrains. Filled with all the amenities the colony lacked. Their tracks had been quickly covered by the shifting of the canyon's black sands.

"He uploaded a map to their wristbands, made sure the vehicles and supplies they brought would be sufficient for their little trip."

"Did he warn them about the Tamal?"

"He did."

"Those idiots headed that way anyway."

Agda shifted her small black eyes to the corner of

the room. The Tamal was a sore subject for the Bethians of the colony. A tribe to the southeast of Colony2, hostile to the colonists and other natives alike, its lands began just beyond a series of rocky buttes. The whispered consensus among the crew was that the Tamal were responsible for the failure of Colony3. Teams from the remaining colonies found the dome structures intact but eerily deserted. Meals were left rotting on their plates. Not a single colonist was found, alive or otherwise. The fate of a hundred settlers remained unknown, officially labeled a Lost Colony. Relations between Colony2's mixed population of humans and Bethians strained with heavy mistrust following the incident.

"We killed our planet and went out to the stars," Neta said, "but instead of working together to create something better, we let the companies take over again. Grabbing anything they could find, stripping and selling planets, just to move further out and do the same to more planets."

Agda stayed silent.

"Were things better before we came?" Neta asked.

"How do you mean?"

"Was this planet better off before we arrived? Did we just turn it into another shitshow?"

"Shitshow?" Agda asked, not knowing the word.

"It means exactly how it sounds," Neta said, scratching at her bandage.

"It sounds disgusting."

"Then you've got the general idea."

Colored lights blinked to life on the other end of the dome, telling the doctor the much-awaited results were ready.

Doctor Canalis pulled a sheet of film from the shiny machine and held it up to the light. It cast a shadow over her alabaster skin and bright eyes. She pressed several buttons on her own wristband. Neta envied her. Not because she was tall and pretty or because she was the only crew member still receiving regular payments, while the rest of the crew simply accrued IOU credits that would be paid out upon purchase of the planet. She envied the doctor because her water rations were prioritized to ensure perfect hygiene. She was clean and smelled nice, really nice actually, like a goddamn field of lavender. Neta would gladly forfeit her week's credits to smell like lavender. She muttered quiet curses to herself, quickly running fingers through her black hair. Flat and greasy compared to Canalis' teased and crimped blonde locks, matching the latest styles seen on stable and populated planets.

The doors slid open, Erickson stamped in, silencing the quick chirps from his wristband. He put a familiar hand on Agda's shoulder, leaned down, and whispered into her ear. She nodded quietly and turned, leaving the room, glancing back quickly at Neta as the doorway closed once again. He stood over Neta silently sneering.

Doctor Canalis began to walk forward, but upon seeing Erickson raging at his Communication Officer, she feigned adjusting settings on her closest piece of equipment.

"This can't be good," Neta said with a smile, attempting to fill the silence.

"You drew your sidearm on the representative of a commercial interest," he scolded.

Neta looked around the room in confusion, taken aback and slightly insulted by his reproach.

"How am I supposed to write this up to the mediators? This is the first sign of interest we've had. If word gets out that a terraformer almost shot a buyer, we will never get another chance at getting off this planet." His voice grew louder with each word until he was yelling, his face turning red.

"You could start by thanking me for diffusing a violent attack," Neta sneered back just as loud, mirroring his anger, "of which there were no actual casualties, excluding myself." She shoved her bandaged forearm into his face.

"Then, you can include the fact that my blaster wasn't even charged. So, no one was in any actual danger of being shot," she continued, "not by me, at least."

"Why wasn't your blaster charged?" he asked, even more annoyed.

Not being the solution Neta was hoping it would be, she shook her head. "Procedures say I have to carry it, nothing about keeping it powered up. There's a better chance the core will explode before I have to ever use it."

"The core isn't going to explode," Erickson said, laughing as the tension broke.

"I heard the company bought them cheap from a star system without regulations."

"That's probably true. The cheap part, but power cores don't explode. It's more like a fizzle and pop."

"Not what I heard." Neta shrugged.

"It doesn't matter," Erickson said, motioning for Doctor Canalis to join them.

"You're staying?" Neta asked. She hopefully reminded herself it wasn't unusual for him to be here, regularly needing to consult with her on colony-related business.

"I asked the Commander to come," the doctor said.

She looked between the serious expressions populating the room. Canalis put the sheet down in the center of a table. "Neta, don't worry," she said in a practiced soothing voice, "it could be worse." Erickson nodded his head from over the doctor's shoulder.

"Ooooh noooo," Neta whispered, deliberately stretching out the words as she took a seat on an exam table, rustling the paper cover of the cushioned table loudly as she adjusted herself.

"Alright. About your arm," the doctor said.

Neta nodded, acknowledging she understood why she had spent the last few hours in the dome.

"The bad news is that we're dealing with an infection. A fungal infection. A pretty aggressive one," she said. She paused to make sure Neta understood. "I'll be honest with you. There is still so much we don't know—that we won't know for a long time—about the pathogens on this planet."

Neta stopped her, shaking her head. "No, I couldn't have gotten it here. I've been careful about that, at least. I follow all of the decontamination procedures."

"It doesn't seem to matter anymore," Erickson stepped in, "it's no secret that the colony is falling apart. It could have been a minor failure in the filters or your environmental suit. There could be small breaches in the seams of the domes that we can't detect."

"An infection. Okay. But that's pretty broad, though. Right?" Neta asked, "I mean, there are a lot of types of infections. Are we talking about the flesh-eating bacteria kind or the itchy foot kind?"

Canalis furrowed her brow and looked over to the commander for direction. He only offered a slight shrug.

"A little of the former. A little of the latter," the doctor told her.

Neta sat forward. "I don't understand," she said. "I feel like there is something major you're just waiting for me to pick up on. I'm not going to. Just tell me what it is that you're not saying." Sweat formed between her clasped hands. The doctor's voice was gentle, but her eyes articulated a more serious turn in the conversation, Neta held them responsible for her growing anxiety.

"The fungal infections we're used to usually live on and in the body, slowly breaking down the host tissue. What we're seeing infects in the same way some viruses do. The spores attack living cells in the host and insert a copy of their DNA, changing the genome of that cell." Canalis paused to make sure Neta understood, mistaking her stunned expression for confusion. "It replaces the host with itself. Turning it into something similar to tree bark."

"Okay, I've got that part," she said.

"There are diseases like it, where healthy tissue is

regrown as bone or hardened tissue. But this is replacing your skin with an alien tissue." Canalis stood and reached for a small bottle. She shook it around gently. "We are calling this Fibrodysplasia Lignum for lack of a better description at this time. Lignum being Latin for wood."

"Fibro..." Neta tried to repeat.

"Fibrodysplasia Lignum."

"Fibrodystatia."

"Dysplasia."

"Lincoln?"

"Lignum."

"We've been calling it the Bark for short," Erickson interrupted, recognizing Neta's defense mechanisms.

Inside the bottle, a splinter of Neta's forearm—broken by the Judge's inhuman grip—clattered against the glass.

"If left untreated, it will spread."

Canalis handed Neta the glass bottle. "How far?" Neta asked, inspecting the fragment.

"Eventually, deeper into the muscle and bone. Up your arm and into your heart and lungs."

Neta itched the bandage. "You mentioned treatment."

"A Capozole injection, cheap and quick, should stop the spread. It won't return the damaged tissue to normal, but it will keep the Bark from spreading"

"Well, let's get to it," Neta said, realizing the other shoe was dropping as she said it.

"We ran through our Capozole supplies months ago," Dr. Canalis said.

"Can you just cut it off?"

"As a last resort. But we'd need to go deep. If you take precautions to slow the spread, we shouldn't need to do anything so risky until supplies arrive.

"Just keep doing what you've been doing," Canalis reassured her, "follow the procedures and limit exposure to the open atmosphere. The more exposure, the more spores, the quicker the progression. Especially avoid any cuts or scrapes, the infection spreads faster through open wounds."

"Alright," Neta said quietly, getting up to leave. She'd left behind a life and family. To what, turn into a tree?

"There's more," Dr. Canalis said, stopping her.

"This is above your rank, so this doesn't leave the room," Erickson told her. "If you speak a word of this to anyone, you forfeit your credits."

"I haven't actually been paid," Neta said.

"This is serious," he said, looking for Dr. Canalis to continue.

"We think about half of the colony has been infected so far," the doctor said. "The Capozole we did have wouldn't have been enough to handle the number currently infected."

"We can all just be trees together," Neta said, "a nice happy forest."

"If word gets out there is an outbreak, we'll have a mutiny," Erickson added. He ushered Neta out of the room. "We know the supply ship in orbit has enough medicine for everyone here. If we just do our jobs, get through this bankruptcy situation, we'll all be fine," he said, standing in front of the circular doorway, waiting as the motors groaned to open.

"We can't wait for this bankruptcy thing to sort itself out," Erickson told Neta, pulling her aside in the tube-shaped hallway that led from the medical dome to the barracks.

"Didn't I hear something about just doing our jobs?"

"It's been almost a month, and nothing has happened. We've only just now had our first appraisers come out. That's not a good sign. Sales can take years to negotiate, and they fall through more often than not. We can't trust that anything is going to change now."

"What are we supposed to do? We can't go to the supply ship. And they're not going to come down to us."

"I'm not talking about the supply ship," Erickson said. He pulled his sleeve back and placed his silver wristbands against a glass wall panel. The display sputtered to life, showing a grainy image.

"The tourists," he said.

"What about the tourists?"

"I verified their supplies before they left. You know what they have?" he asked, scrolling through a digital list. Finally, he stopped and flipped the image around for Neta to see.

"Capozole." She read out loud.

"That's right. We can go out there. Find them and buy it," he said. "I have enough credits stashed away. You help me find them and your dose will be your payment."

"Why don't we just wait until they come back?

Why go out there and risk it?"

Erickson unzipped his jumpsuit and pulled the side of his top over to expose his chest. Neta expected to see muscular definition and dark hair, but it was smooth, replaced with the ashy green shell and flaking brown strips of bark, like the aspen trees back home. She hadn't been wealthy enough to play among the few remaining trees in the private gardens where they grew, but she had been clever enough to get in anyway, dissatisfied with only sneaking glances at the canopies that rose over the protective walls.

"I don't have time," he said, quickly zipping up his top, glancing around to make sure nobody had seen. "Doc says the Bark is making its way for my heart."

"I'm sorry," Neta said through gritted teeth.

"When is the tower going to be operational?" Erickson asked.

"Everything is all set for it to go back up first thing in the morning."

"If we're going to do this, I need you to delay it. Any communication will be added to the official logs, and this has to be kept off the books.

Neta reformatted the servers she had configured to handle the communications system, erasing the work she had already begun. Even if the Bethians were able to get the tower repositioned on schedule, the systems would remain down for another day. Erickson announced over the Colony2 intercom system that because of the delay in re-establishing the systems, the Communications Officer and he would be traveling to Colony1 to establish physical contact.

The sky was unkissed by the red moon when they loaded up early the next morning. They snuck like thieves through the dark. Only the lights from their wristbands and the headlights of the landrockets illuminated their preparation, their deception leaving them in quiet guilt.

"How will we know where to find them?" Neta asked. "Without the comms tower, we won't be able to ping their locations."

"I gave them directions to the ruttlehorn grounds closest to the World Builder they wanted to examine. We'll go there first."

"So that's why they went toward the Stacks."

"They know not to go too far that way, and the Tamal have been quiet lately. I don't think they'll have an issue."

"Hrmm," Neta grunted, sipping her three-day-old coffee from her pack, flavorless except for a watered-down bitterness.

"That's not water, is it?" Erickson asked.

"Most of it is by now," Neta said.

"Why do you do that to yourself?"

"I don't like the way the air tastes from these filters," Neta said. "Too electric."

Erickson made a final confirmation the fuel cells were fully charged. The landrockets were little more than disarmed missiles: long metal cylinders sitting upon a pair of landing skis, a leather saddle, and a simple handlebar to control everything from steering and acceleration to ascent. Near the rear thrusters, two squares flanked either side. Ambiguous tubes ran in and out of the boxes, serving a purpose Neta could merely guess at. Cool air entered in through a turbine at the front of the rocket and converted into propellant. Neta had ridden a landrocket only once in her short time at Colony2. She was not a fan.

"Are you ready?" Erickson asked.

Neta waited. She wanted to say something about safety and other possibilities, but she knew both time and options were limited. She nodded in confirmation. She hoisted herself into the saddle, resting her feet in a set of metal stirrups that hung from leather straps.

"Here we go," he said, boiling sand into the air as he accelerated past the beehive-shaped huts. Neta watched as the landing skis ascended into the belly of his rocket. Her own landrocket sputtered as it started, kicking back a burst of dark smoke. She followed from a distance, uneasily steering her rocket out of his rear-flank, avoiding the spray against her helmet. They climbed and dropped with the shifting dunes surrounding the colony, never rising more than a few meters above the surface. They had only been traveling a short time but were already out of the range of the colony's short-range radio.

"You managing alright back there?"

"I'm fine,"

"Like to take a break?"

"I would have liked a vehicle that was more land-based," she said, the black desert floor passing in the limited visibility of her headlights, a galaxy of reflective pebbles flowing beneath.

"We make do with what we've got. Anyway, we can cover the distance quicker than their ShuttleCrawler."

They rode the landrockets hard through the predawn hours. At length, their path weaved through natural stone pillars and arches marking the end of the black desert, where the meteor that would become Intiloch made its deepest impact. Slowly the landscape subsided into pockets of tall grassy reeds, their roots reaching far down to drink from water buried deep underground.

Even in the deepest gorges, there was no water on the planet. The reeds drank from the subsurface streams, providing the Bethians and a few other species with food and the low-hanging atmosphere that blanketed the canyon. The Cornflower Mining Corporation had planned to do to Beth what they had done to dozens of other rogue planets: quickly strip the outer layers of the crust of valuable resources and leave when its surface became too volatile. Those plans changed when the survey team discovered safety in the valley, allowing them to terraform a habitable colony. They would be able to mine longer and deeper, to access rare minerals that formed following the celestial impact. All of it was now waiting patiently for new legal landholders to mine and export out to the galaxy.

The patches eventually converged, forming a great lake of dusty reeds, covering the canyon floor further than Neta could see.

"We go over, it takes too long to go around," Erickson said over the short-wave.

"This isn't like you," she said, following him over the reeds, the thick stalks bending as they passed.

"How do you reckon?"

"You don't seem like the type to break protocol, especially when it's your own."

"What makes you think you know me?" he asked. "And what protocol am I breaking, exactly?"

"I've known a lot of people like you. I was in the Class Wars. That shouldn't be a surprise. Everyone within Earth-proximity was. I was just on the losing side. It should be in my file."

"It is. You were listed as a 'Non-Combatant.'"

"I'm not much of a fighter, got caught delivering sandwiches to a safehouse."

Erickson laughed unexpectedly.

"Yeah, it's really funny," Neta said defensively.

"No, you say you're not much of a fighter, but you did just point a gun at someone yesterday."

"An unloaded gun. That's different. That's not fighting. And that's not my point. There were women and men like you. Who would do anything for the people they led. Give up their meals in the prison camps. Make a big sacrifice in the field, if you know what I mean." Neta said.

"And you think I'm being selfish?" Erickson asked.

"I don't know if selfish is the right word," Neta said.

"It's alright. You're free to your opinions, and you're not wrong. But there are no protocols about not being selfish."

"Maybe not a written rule. But in my opinion, when the Commander and Communications Officer of the only remaining colony come begging for medicine, maybe their planet doesn't look like a very smart investment. Especially when one of them pointed a gun in your face just yesterday."

"We're not begging. We're buying," Erickson said. "And we don't know what happened to Colony1. They could have gotten missed by the storm."

"Coming out here could kill everyone else's chance of getting the help they need."

"Everyone else has more time than I do. Doc says I'm looking at days or weeks at best before a piece of Bark hits an artery. The fact of the matter is, I just want to live. Simple as that," he said, "I want to grow old, have kids."

"And you'll need to get off this planet to do that," Neta said.

Erickson was quiet for a second. "Not necessarily," he said in a whisper. She could hear his smile, like a child happy to have a secret they were excited to share.

"You've got pretty slim pickings out here," Neta said. "Who're you thinking, Canalis?"

"No, it isn't the Doc."

"You don't mean—" Neta trailed off, worried he was speaking about her. Lolo's daughter was too young for the commander—she hoped—and there were few other women at the colony. The list wouldn't be long before it reached her name.

"Agda," Erickson said before Neta could embarrass herself.

"What? Agda? Our Agda? Short, red, looks kind of like an armadillo?" Neta released the accelerator. The sudden loss of speed caused the landrocket to swerve. She over-adjusted, darting quickly off-course. Neta gritted her teeth and pulled against the skid to reorient, taking her time to compose herself.

"I know how it sounds. We've been keeping it quiet. She's probably the most genuine person I've ever met. She has a beautiful soul."

"Yeah, okay. But how would that even work? Kids. You two don't even have the same type of skeletons. You wouldn't be able to— The parts don't— How?"

"Not that our relationship is lacking in passion—"

"Oh god. Nevermind. I don't want to know."

"—but we'll need to get a geneticist. Doc doesn't see a reason why humans and Bethians shouldn't be able to make something viable."

"A geneticist is going to cost you."

"Like I told you, I have some credits saved up. We're not looking for a designer baby. We just want what everyone wants: happy and healthy," Erickson said. "Would you rather it was the Doc?"

"No, actually." Though Neta was relieved to find she wasn't the subject of his affection, she would have considered it a loss in her imagined rivalry if Canalis had been the recipient.

She looked to a glowing sliver above the western canyon wall. "We're finally going to be getting daylight." She could feel the morning air that whipped through her jumpsuit beginning to warm. The static of the moon's interference hummed in their radios. Ahead of them, the prairie gave way to branching rivers of the thick grasses following their water source. The streams cut into valleys, giving way to the highland of mossy hills and rocky low mountains. The outlines of the faraway Arid Mountains appeared in the distance like skeletons.

"Right. If we get separated, follow the reeds," Erickson said. "That's where the ruttlehorns will gather. Our guests will be staying close."

"Shit," Neta said, her landrocket sputtering again as it did during departure. This time the smoke was darker, coming from the end and neither it nor the shaking would stop. Her control over the vehicle waned. Jostling in her saddle, she coaxed the missile down onto a mossy patch of ground, just past the headwaters and between a split in two lengths of reeds.

"Everything alright back there?" Erickson asked, making a wide circle around.

"I don't think this one is going any further," Neta said. She dismounted and gave the cylinder a hard kick, then unlatched a side-panel to the landrocket's rudimentary mechanics. More smoke poured out of the opening, denser and darker than the smoke pouring out of the ends. Out of instinct, she fanned it away from her glass helmet.

Erickson dropped his rocket onto its landing skis beside her.

"We'll have to leave it. We don't have any tools or any way to fix it right here. Just have to come back for it later, I guess."

"Your rocket will seat two?" Neta asked.

"Not comfortably, but it will," he said.

"Fantastic."

Something darted between them from out of the reeds, a shrubrat. Unlike the tumbleweed Neta had seen the day before, this one was more rat than shrub, its face a loose patchwork of leather hanging over a long snout and a mouth filled with small sharp teeth. Its small eyes sat far back, almost on its neck where its torso formed a hard segmented shell and underside in a thick evolutionary precursor to fur. From out of the armor, small green tendrils ran upward, slowly greying as they connected to form a sprout of feathery leaves. Quickly, it fled in terror, its life disrupted by the landrockets passing over the lake, an apocalyptic event for its tiny brain.

"We need to go," Erickson said, his voice immediately stern, "now."

A series of high-pitched squeaks grew from where it had exited the reeds. The sound grew steadily until hundreds of panicked chirps bled into a singularity. Neta looked back to see the reeds closest to her begin to shake.

"Get on, now!" he screamed. She followed his orders and crammed herself into the saddle behind him. Neta wrapped her arms tightly around his torso. Pushing her helmet into the back of his air filter, she tried to turn her head to fit better into the space; the roundness of the globe proved this to be futile.

Erickson was already speeding off before Neta could confirm she was secure. Just as quickly, the reeds opened to release a torrent of shrubrats in various states of shrubbery. The propulsion of the landrocket pushed back against the frontline of creatures, leaving a cloud of spores and moss in their wake. In a few short seconds, they caught up to and overtook the harbinger of the herd. Neta watched, her head still tilted against Erickson's back, as they quickly passed over.

"That one's still young," Erickson said, "the Bark hasn't gotten much of a grip on it yet."

"Bark?" Neta asked.

"According to the Doc, the mess of leaves coming out of their backs, the spores it releases. That's where it comes from."

"Why doesn't the Bark kill them?"

"It does, just not as quickly as it does us."

A blue flare rose over the low mountain crest laying before them. The light of burning phosphorus climaxed and briefly hung weightless in the canyon air before falling. As best she could tell, it had been fired directly to the left of the trail they had been following. Erickson twisted the handles of the landrocket in pursuit of the beacon. A safe distance away, the southeastern Stacks marking the territory of the Tamal tribe peaked over the horizon line.

When they reached the top of the hill, Erickson set the rocket down on the skis and pulled back. A set of front-facing thrusters ignited, pitching them to a stop. Erickson dismounted, running at a frantic sprint. He was already halfway to the bottom of the hill. Over the radio, he yelled something Neta couldn't hear, about something she couldn't see. She slid forward in the saddle and twisted the handles of the rocket. The vehicle punched forward, sliding across the summit of the stone hill, skis bouncing along the uneven surface. Another slight twist of the handles and the rocket pushed over and down the hill, sparks crackling white hot in her wake.

Neta caught up to Erickson as he pulled a blaster from its holster. She lifted herself from the seat and stepped in line behind the Commander. A trail of slickened moss led from a thicket of reeds to a solitary ShuttleCrawler. Neta and Erickson approached slowly from the opposite side, cautious of the muffled grunting from within. Erickson stepped around the recreational vehicle's slanted front and peered through the divided windshields. The vehicle was empty. The noise hadn't come from inside but from behind. Neta crouched down, looking under the vehicle. She could see a shape—one of the visitors—seated up against a rear set of folded mechanical legs.

"On the other side," she said in a whisper, waving two fingers at Erickson, motioning him to go around. He lifted his eyebrow in agreement, stepping slowly and pointing his gun forward as he rounded the corner. Quickly the weapon dropped back into its holster. The trail of darkened moss led to Eddy, the black-mustachioed tourist Neta had drawn her depleted blaster on in the commissary. He lay wheezing, blood overflowing from a series of golf ball-sized holes arranged in a circle around his gut.

"What did this?" Neta asked.

"Ruttlehorn," Erickson said.

As if summoned by its name, the beast bound out from the thicket of reeds. With each step, a slurry of droning notes—a garbled organ tune—played through the crown of horns on top of its head. Dull eyes locked upon Neta, gnashing human-like teeth from a long lipless mouth. At some point, either before or after the goring, Eddy had managed to fire a shot into the creature's shoulder.

Erickson again reached for his holstered blaster,

but his draw took too long. If the ruttlehorn had been in better condition, it would have been faster and done to them what it had done to the tourist. A ribbon blast of violet plasma shot between them from a rifle that Eddy held in one hand, its stock propped against the wheel. The laser ripped through the center of the ruttlehorn's crown. Thick, flat feet fell out from under it, the scaled body crashed to the ground spraying dust into the air. Eddy dropped the rifle and slumped forward, his jumpsuit heavy with blood.

"Help me get him inside," Erickson said, grabbing Eddy's arms. His chest lifted with a deep groan. He spasmed at the touch, trying to fight off his would-be rescuers but in too much pain to be moved. The strength left his arms. Neta grabbed his legs. Together they hoisted him up. Slowly they stumbled to the opposite side of the craft, almost dragging Eddy across the ground. The holes in his stomach pooled with dark blood.

Eddy gasped, his eyes fighting to stay open.

"Just hang on," she said, turning her head to reassure him.

Whiteness filled the front of Neta's helmet, blindingly bright. A streak burnt across her vision and stayed there. The light was followed by the familiar electric crack of the atmosphere expanding from the intense and sudden heat. She'd been shot at, not a warning, but a kill shot. It had missed her when she turned her head, but just barely.

Her instincts kicked in. She chose flight. It was every woman for herself. She clawed and climbed over the injured man, using him as a springboard to propel herself into the vehicle. He collapsed onto the rocks and moss outside.

Erickson dropped the canister of patching foam meant to hold Eddy together. He hadn't even looked for the Capozole. He grabbed Neta by the injured arm and pulled her out of the doorway. She screamed, a combination of pain and fear. Another ray of weaponized light passed between her scrambling legs. She fell against a cabinet door. No matter how hard or how many times she blinked, her vision refused to focus. A streak of distortion ran at a diagonal through the center of her line of sight.

"I can't see," she said, holding her gloved hand up to her face.

Erickson grabbed her by the forearm and pulled her arm out of the way to look for himself. "You're fine. Your eyes are fine. The plasma bolt melted your helmet."

Neta looked down. The band didn't follow. She calculated where the shot had come, using the angle of the streak. "Up along the ridge."

Erickson picked a rifle from a gun rack bolted to the wall. He quickly looked it over, the core gently humming awake in his hands as it powered up. He kneeled and set himself up around the corner of the doorframe, presenting as small of a target as his bubble would allow. He closed one eye and looked down the scope, propping the muzzle on a counter. Ahead of him, the canyon floor was a cascading series of bluffs. He scanned each level like steps on a ladder.

"It's the other two, Rob and Judge," he said, "I recognize the jumpsuits, I can almost make out Rob's hair. See if you can get them on the short-wave."

Neta's heart went cold as she flipped through the channels on her wristband. "It's not 'the Judge'?" she asked, trying to hide her fear.

"It's just Judge. It's a name, not a title."

"Are you sure?"

"Pretty sure," Erickson said.

Neta called maydays as she scanned frequencies. More shots tore through the frame of the vehicle, searching for a target. No other answer came over the radio, only the rise and fall of static, the sounds of the violent moon.

"I'm returning fire." Erickson steadied his sights, adjusted slightly for the drop, and moved his finger to the trigger. A shot rang out. Erickson's helmet shattered and exploded out, like a snow globe dropped to the floor. The visitors were quicker, more experienced shots.

Neta stared through the open space where his head had been, not believing what she was seeing through the warped front of her visor. She quickly realized the truth as Erickson's body fell backward. His hand slapped against the rubber padded flooring, knocking his finger against the trigger. The round he had meant to fire at Rob went wild, just missing Neta and into the back bunks of the ShuttleCrawler.

The shot hit something important. "The fuel cells," Neta said to no one. Blue flames spewed out of the back, quickly filling the rest of the vehicle. She attempted to cover her face and push herself toward the first aid kit and reach the Capozole. It was already too late. The medicine was engulfed in a wall of flowing fire. The Bark that was slowly turning her into an alien shrub had quickly become an afterthought.

She turned back to the front of the SRV, pausing at the threshold of the doorway. She took a deep breath of crisp electric air and flung herself past the opening. Another shot fired, and for the third time missed her. She fell through the cockpit, over the driver seat, crawling out the front door. She laid out on the cushioning surface of moss. She wanted to bury herself beneath it but knew she couldn't stop moving. Soon the flames would fill the rest of the vehicle. Any second there could be an explosion. She needed distance and cover from the raining bolts of colored light.

Neta pulled herself to her feet, toward the thicket of reeds while frantically looking over her shoulder, making sure to keep the burning cruiser between her and the shooters. She ducked low as she entered the vegetation, plunging through the thick stalks. She kept pushing through, falling to a crawl, until the reeds thinned on the opposite end. Beyond the few remaining meters, she could see the drop-off to another staircase of ridges. She was certain that they knew where she was by the movement of the plants, swaying as she inched forward.

She was too fast, too far away. Rob took the shot anyway.

"You're not going to miss," he said, demanding the best from himself, no matter what.

"Yes, you are," a baritone crackled over the radio.

Judge was trying to get under his skin, to rattle him for no other reason than his own amusement. He did this constantly, tried to ruin an otherwise fun trip. They hadn't been upset or surprised when his ShuttleCrawler split away from theirs. Hadn't said a word, simply gone on his way. His presence was unsettling, made worse that he was close but unseen. Rob believed he'd had a chance with the kitchen girl, if not for Judge. How could he not have? His hair had been on point, and you wouldn't believe what some of these outer rim girls are willing to do for a few packets of dried food. Especially for a guy flying a StarHopper. The bald creep standing in the corner and staring at everyone put her off the whole group of them. He didn't even need those thick glasses.

Judge was right, of course. She leaped across the ravine with the grace and confidence that comes with having the home-field advantage. His shot tore into the edge where she had been just moments earlier. A stream of small rocks poured down. If she had stopped where she landed, instead of sprinting on, he could have had her. He would have mounted her gorgeous head over his mantle.

The ruttlehorn glanced back at him. Its knowing eyes looked out from under its crown of long blow horns, mocking him. Quickly, it dropped over the horizon and disappeared. He lamented the loss of the trophy.

The radio crackled again. "...got me," another voice said, the beginning cut-off by the static. In the words, there was panic and pain. The only emotions Judge expressed were apathy and rage, nothing between.

He turned around and scanned the morning skyline, watching as the flare rose and fell out of sight.

"I'm coming, Eddy." Rob took his blaster rifle and ran, his helmet bouncing loosely with each step. He pulled up a display of the planet's map uploaded to his wristband by the terraforming crew. His finger drew a straight line between himself and the cruiser, where Eddy had been heading. He zoomed in. A stack of mountain ridges lay between him and his destination. It would take too long to find a new route. He would have to climb down.

Another shot fired off. The SRV was below him now. A battered landrocket parked nearby. They weren't alone. He called Eddy's name over the radio one more time.

"Shush," was the reply he finally received back. It was almost a whisper, but he recognized the voice. It wasn't Eddy. Halfway down the rows of ridges, he found Judge sprawled out on the ground, his pack positioned in front of him, a makeshift stand to stabilize his rifle.

Rob dropped the remaining distance down to where Judge lay and crawled to the edge. Judge's helmet lay between them in the dust.

"You're not worried about getting sick?" he asked.

"Never been sick a day in my life," Judge said, "I shoot better without it anyway."

"Shooting at what?" he asked.

Judge nodded toward the SRV. Rob looked down the scope of his rifle. He recognized Eddy's jumpsuit; blood stained the front and weighed down the back where it pooled. He was being dragged by two figures from around the rear of the cruiser. They stopped at the entrance, clad in the signature light blue of the now-defunct Cornflower operation.

"I warned you boys about messing around with locals. There's a good reason terraformers have a reputation. You don't take a job like that if you have any other options," Judge said with a sneer.

"A robbery gone wrong?" Rob asked.

"I've seen some troubled crews before. These colonists have been marooned for too long. They reek of desperation. Desperate people do desperate things." One of the locals disappeared into the ShuttleCrawler. "Eddy must have caught them breaking in for supplies." The lone figure kneeled beside the corpse.

Judge said nothing. He added just a few pounds of pressure to the trigger, giving Rob no warning. His target moved her head. The beam brushed past the helmet as it shifted. Judge cursed. Their luck on this planet was lousy, and the element of surprise was gone. He reset the rifle, waiting a second for the next charge to be ready. When he looked back, set to fire, his target had disappeared through the doorway. Judge fired several rounds into the SRV, hopeful a lucky shot would connect.

"No matter how they try to escape, they need to go past that doorway. Anything moves, you shoot. We've got them trapped."

"I see you," Rob whispered, eyeing a rifle leveling in his direction. He recognized the chump who escorted them out of the colony. Rob took the shot first.

"Good shot. A clean kill. Better than he deserved," Judge opined.

Exogeny

The other thief jumped past the doorway. This time his shot didn't hit. They'd be going through the front door, out of his view.

"Go after her. I'll cover you from up here," Judge told him.

Rob looked over the edge. He estimated about a dozen feet down to the next drop. The SRV burst into flames. That bitch was trying to strand them. He jumped the distance. Through the flames, he could see her racing towards a grove of reeds. The locals were smarter than he had given them credit for. They had been told to stay close to the brush. No doubt, easier to keep track of their movements. It just so happened that their communications network was down. There were too many coincidences. A conspiracy designed the instant of their arrival. He leaped down the remaining ridges.

When Rob was far enough away, Judge plucked a still wet lump of chewing gum from where it had stuck on the side of his gun and placed it back in his mouth. He picked up his pack, slung his rifle over his shoulder, and secured his helmet before beginning the climb up the ridge back to his ShuttleCrawler.

"Rob are you there?" came the voice over the radio. A woman's voice. Rob recognized it from the attack in the colony's commissary. This one wasn't nearly as cute as the chef's daughter, but she was alright. He wondered if she was the one to make the shot that killed his friend. She had been awfully quick to point a blaster at Eddy.

"I'm here," he responded, rifle tight against his shoulder. He stepped toward the raging bonfire that had been their transportation, purchased and paid for by his father's company. The insurance paperwork was going to take forever to fill out. Carefully, he approached the body, slumped on the ground just out of the flames reach. He pulled it a little further, just to be safe. His wife would want it returned for a proper burial. Small grey tendrils emerged from the holes in Eddy's chest. Saplings.

"What the hell did you do to him?"

"There's been some kind of misunderstanding," she said.

"Help me understand then, darlin'." His voice taking on the southern drawl Eddy used to instigate her in the colony's commissary. He came around the side of the cruiser, finding the remains of the ruttlehorn. He knelt next to the creature, keeping his rifle pointed to the reeds. He tried to recreate the scene. That must have been the first shot he heard, Eddy dropping the creature. Not a very clean shot—definitely Eddy—it wouldn't have made a very good trophy.

"We didn't come here to hurt anyone," she told him.

"But you did anyway." Slowly he moved into the reeds, moving the thick plants out of his way with the barrel of the gun.

"We didn't do anything to Eddy, he was gored by a ruttlehorn."

He paused to listen. A faint whirring noise led him forward. The sound of an old air filter that no longer ran silently. It got louder as he moved closer.

"Please," she begged in a whisper. "I don't know what you think you saw."

Exogeny

Between the reeds, light reflected off of a round glass helmet. Slowly he raised his rifle.

Helmetless, Neta shoved into Rob's back, the stalks cutting across her bare face. She pushed her entire body into him, aiming low at his center of gravity. She had learned to be tricky as a child, to win without fighting, when bigger children would try to take what little she had. It had served her well in the war. She hadn't had anyone to rely on back then either. She used all of the force she could muster. It was too much. Together they went over the edge.

This ridge was higher than the others. Two times, maybe three times higher. Neta felt the tightening of her stomach drop, clusters of nerves all activating at once. Rob hit the ground first, his chest producing a sickeningly wet crunch with the impact. Her shoulder fell into his pack, the rest of her landed on top of him, a hard cushion.

The glass cracked. His helmet hit a large grey stone, crumpling inward instead of shattering thanks to a thin layer of plastic coating. Neta had killed him. She didn't need to check. His body twitched with tiny spasms. She hadn't killed anyone before. Not even during the war. She had seen enough bodies to know. She tried not to look at him, tried not to breathe or gasp. She only rolled over and picked herself up, trying to hold her breath, her helmet left in the stalks above where it had acted as her decoy.

Rob's back faced towards the sky, and she wrestled with his supply pack, struggling to get his limp arms to pull free. Neta and Erickson didn't bring supplies of their own. He'd feared it would have been too suspect to the other colonists if they intended to reach Colony1 before nightfall. She needed what was in that pack. She looked at the ridge she stood on, where Rob lay dead. There was no way off except up or down. Sharp pain in her shoulder told her she wouldn't be going up. In the distance, the World Builder stood tall before her.

When active, the World Builder was a display of hypnotic lights and the pulsing bass of industrial filters and matter converters, siphoning and transforming Beth's atmosphere. Neta had seen it only once. Now and ever since the Cornflower Mining Company's bankruptcy, it rested quietly. A mechanical ghost town, abandoned and hollow. Oval-shaped and asymmetrical on the horizontal axis—like a massive upside-down egg—the terraforming engine stands high in the valley upon three mechanical legs, dwarfed only by the natural black stone columns that lay just beyond, the Stacks marking the boundary of the Tamal territory. Neta ran as fast as she could through the open highlands, for the refuge the World Builder could provide, believing the Judge was only steps behind or waiting in some hidden cavern. He never showed.

Taking only shallow breaths, she pulled on the unrelenting access hatch. It was at least a minute before she saw the thin metallic line sealing the doorframe, welded shut to prevent any sabotage from the nearby tribe. She climbed back down the ladder of the support leg. Directly below the apex of the egg, Neta found a dense ring of stone outcroppings pushed out from the surface by the vibrations and heat of the terraformer. She unfolded the small tent from Rob's pack in the center of the ring, hoping to remain hidden by anyone unfamiliar with the terrain.

Cross-legged, Neta sat in the stolen tent, too short to stand in but just long enough for her to lay. The pack only included the essentials. At her side lay Rob's rifle. A small filter cleaned the air silently as she triple-checked the half-empty first aid kit, a tin containing some bandages, mild painkillers that had done little to dull the pain in her shoulder, and a can of patching foam, the kind they had been looking to find for Eddy before everything went to hell. It had been foolish of Erickson to think they would have been able to save him with a bit of patching foam, not with how insistent his blood had been about filling up all the wrong places. Erickson was dead now too. She hadn't taken a moment until now to process anything that had occurred since she got off the landrocket.

She checked Rob's first aid kit one last time, spilling its contents out onto the floor of the tent. Still no Capozole. The supply would have been in his crawler, gone up in flames.

"What do I tell Agda?" she asked herself. She had no answer. There were going to be so many others that needed explanations: the mediator, the rest of their crew. They'd had no reason to be in the middle of the canyon instead of their stated destination of Colony1. Any excuse she could come up with didn't include revealing an infection of space fungus was slowly turning them into trees.

She hadn't known Erickson long, but she felt like she should cry. She tried tightening her eyelids to force the smallest amount of moisture from her tear ducts. If she could just give it a little push, maybe the rest would follow. She failed.

"How can you not cry for someone you just saw murdered?" she said, berating herself. She tried picturing the event; Erickson's head was there, then it wasn't. She had made sure not to look too hard, even as she leaped over his corpse to escape the fire and blaster shots. Again, she failed. Instead, she only made herself angry—at herself, the misunderstanding, and the tourists who had shot at them so casually.

"At least I got one of theirs." She felt her throat tighten like a fist at the words, an immediate burning in her esophagus. She had killed someone. They hadn't killed Eddy, but she had killed Rob. Not entirely on purpose, but it happened. It was him or me, she told herself. She had tried to explain, but he hadn't listened. She had to do it if she ever wanted to leave this planet, she repeated. She kept repeating it, but it only helped to stop the stomach acid from rising in her throat.

"Even if I were able to leave, where could I go?" She asked. There was so much to answer for on Beth, and she had burnt so many bridges on Earth. She pushed the thought out of her head and took a deep breath.

Neta dumped the rest of the pack onto the pile of bandages: several condensed meal bars, a small rubber bladder of water, and a roll of cloth tape. She tore the top of the water pack off, drinking deeply, realizing how thirsty she was. In between gulps, she tore off strips of the cloth tape. The leafy offshoots of the reeds had cut through her jumpsuit like tiny razors. She applied the tape to the already stitched-together suit. It wouldn't matter much without her helmet and filter.

She removed the glove from her infected hand, a thin oblong something fell out into her lap. It was the size of a small coin, opaque white with a slight yellow tinge. At first, Neta believed it to be another splinter of the Bark on her arm, chipped off in the commotion. She held it up, there was something familiar about it, the curve and shape, the slight rigidity of the wider end. It was a fingernail. Immediately, she gagged and dropped it. She checked her hand, sure enough, her index finger stood bare like a fleshy sausage. She poked at it gently with her healthy hand, fully expecting the sting of freshly exposed nerves. She felt nothing at all.

"Maybe only half an hour," she said. She hadn't been exposed long but already the rash on her arm had grown larger and harder, the same ashy green color she had seen on Erickson's chest. Where it had cracked in the Judge's grip was no longer bleeding or raw, the ruptures sealed and filled with more Bark. The motion in her wrist was noticeably limited as if she had slept on top of it. She moved it around in small circles to help it loosen up, to no avail. The border between skin and disease had begun to itch, she wasn't sure if it had always felt that way or if she just imagined it, hoping to retain some feeling.

She would need to retrace her steps, she thought. Find her helmet and landrocket. It would need to wait until morning. She was still too sore from her fall to climb the ridges back where she had left them.

Checking her handiwork, she held up the repaired suit. "Flashlight on," she commanded. The beam scanned over the suit, searching for any missed cuts or tears, finding none. A slight twist of a dial and the light flickered away while a gallery of images appeared on the screen. A short video played, a young girl, olive-skinned with dark hair, still a baby. Neta watched the child begin taking clumsy steps towards the camera.

Outside the tent, something hit another something. A rock being kicked. Neta turned the wristband off and listened. One of the things was moving slowly. The Judge had come looking, she thought. Perhaps another ruttlehorn. Her lungs stopped in panic. She was sure her heart would quickly follow. A monster had found her. There were more noises, less cautious now. It wasn't him, she realized. There was more than one thing, now dozens of somethings.

Slowly, Neta reached for the rifle at her side. She was sure she could get a shot off, maybe scare the unseen things away. Shadows fell over the eastern wall where they blocked the sun from the tent's side, but the footsteps now circled her completely. She raised the gun at one of the shadows and squeezed the trigger. The violet laser blast burnt a small, clean hole the size of her fist through the wall of the tent, but she couldn't tell if she had hit her target.

"Should have switched to shotgun mode," she said

regretfully.

Her preemptive attack did not frighten the shadows away. They rushed forward. The walls of the tent pushed in from all directions, caving in and grasping her tightly. She kicked blindly, pushing off several attackers. They were replaced with more bodies, squeezing her harder. She felt the tent lifting off the ground, followed by a sharp blow to the back of her head.

"Was that a rock?" she asked as the walls caved in and faded to black. Neta fell into an involuntary sleep.

Neta dreamed of the wooden rocking chair that her mother and grandmother had sat in when she was a child. The real chair had not survived to Neta's adulthood, lost when a Bougee missile landed in their apartment. Now, she sat in their place, her daughter in her arms. She looked at the child. Hot tears she couldn't account for stung Neta's face, wiped raw by the sleeve of her sweater. Her daughter still glowed the pink complexion of a newborn. Heavy and warm, her skin still smelled blissfully saccharine. They had been trying to nurse for weeks, but nothing had come naturally to mother or child. Something was missing between them. A synapse that never connected.

"Please," Neta begged, "you need to eat."

It was easy to blame the child, but Neta was sure the problem was herself. It couldn't be anyone else's fault. The baby was, after all, just a baby and very small. This was—somehow—her fault too. She was supposed to be good at this, right? Ancestrally inherited knowledge or instincts lost in recessive genes. She was haunted by paranoia that those around could see her guilt.

It had been days since Neta had slept. She watched herself, as if from outside her own body, growing irritable. She hated how she treated the father and those around her, who were only offering their help. Each time she took her frustrations out on them, it only made her madder and more irrational. She didn't want to hurt her baby, but she was incapable of providing the most basic necessity and safety.

The baby opened her soft mouth. Neta knew what the reply would be. Her child would tell her, "You are a failure as a woman. A failure at the one thing your mothers before you had all mastered."

But only a muffled yell escaped, bubbling forth as if they were underwater. Neta gasped as the muted yellow nursery fell away, leaving her and her daughter sitting in darkness, with only the realization that there had never been a yellow nursery on the planet Beth. The baby's mouth opened again. The yell grew louder, coming to the surface, proclaiming her name. The color of the child's deep brown eyes faded into the same blackness that surrounded them. She could see through the face of her daughter and into the vastness of space. Again, the shouting became clearer. "Neta." The voice didn't belong to the child.

A pair of slender fingers wrapped around the child. Exactly how those same fingers had encircled Mr. Lolo's head in the commissary. They lifted the child away. Neta pushed forward to rise from her seat but

Exogeny

was pulled back. Powerless to stop it, her limbs heavy, refusing to move. The Judge held the babe in front of his thin white face, smirking his empty expression. Slowly, they too fell away into the darkness of space, following the room and disappearing in the blackness. Neta knew then, nothing she did would hurt the child the way that men like him could. And there were many men like him. Could she get it back, she wondered. Would things be better now if she could?

She struggled to chase after, finding her arms grafted to her Grandmother's chair, melted into the wood itself. The Bark had spread.

"Wake up," yelled the voice from out of the darkness. Neta spilled onto the hand-hewn stone, dumped from her stolen tent by a crew of Bethians. She tried to pick herself up in a nauseous panic but fell flat. Even though she felt the open air on her face, she could not orient between the sky and the ground. The horizon in front of her swung across her vision, dizzying and confusing. Stricken by newfound claustrophobia, her breath went short.

"Who's there?" she called out loudly, bare stone cool on her side and face. The light of the moon stabbed down on her spinning head.

"Calm down," the Judge ordered coldly. She vomited when she saw him, heaved until nothing was left.

"Where?" she asked after her empty stomach stopped retching.

"Not sure." The Judge looked around. "The top of a temple," he said matter-of-factly.

Neta opened her eyes to take in the surroundings. From what she could tell, it was pyramid-like in shape, the top flattened and encircled by roughly carved pillars. It towered in the middle of sprawling concentric circles of beehive-shaped huts, woven from dried reeds. Rounded outlying appendages of longhouses lined the borders of the city, forming a vast mandala. By the number of huts, she guessed there would have to be hundreds of them, but the streets were silent and empty. She spat, clearing her mouth of stomach acid saliva. "Bethian," she said. "A tribe that's never been too friendly. They call themselves Tamals." The man nodded.

She fought the spinning in her head. The Judge was bound, hands tied to a stake. He had managed to sit up, his face bruised blue and smeared with dried blood from a cut running front-to-back over the right side of his bald scalp.

The Bethians who had dropped her had disappeared. Around them, the pillars were left unguarded, wide open. She knew she was in no shape to stand, much less make a run for it. The Judge could have simply walked out and down any of the sets of stairs on each of the four sides if not for the stake that held him firmly in place. Through the openings, Neta could see a dark cloud growing in the distance.

"That was Rob's tent they pulled you out of. I take it you got the drop on him too?" he said in his unaffected baritone, reminding Neta they were unshielded from the outside world, space fungus included. Neta wondered how long she had been asleep, how much the Bark had spread.

"Where's my stuff?" she asked.

Exogeny

The Judge nodded to a longhouse at the bottom of the stone steps. "They brought us through the big one before dropping us off. Left everything in there."

"Capozole?" she asked, avoiding his question.

"What?"

"An antifungal injection." Her wrist was bent forward, locked in place. Stop. It's just in your head, she thought, just calm down. Still, it refused to move back into a natural position. She rolled over onto her knees, balled into a fetal position on the stone floor, still too dizzy to lift her head. She pulled her arms under her, grabbed the open fist with her good hand, and pushed it back. The joint creaked, like an old dresser drawer moving against its frame, wood grinding against wood.

"I know what it is. What about it?"

"Is there any in your pack? Do you have any?" she clarified, nodding to his pack.

"No, it'd be in my ShuttleCrawler."

"Where?"

"Jesus. It's not going to do you any good. Last time I saw it was before you did in Eddy. These little savages got the drop on me. I dropped my fair share of them, though. I'll kill the rest before I'm done here." He curled his lip. Neta couldn't tell if it was excitement, or anger, or a perverse combination. "Then we'll see what I do to your den of thieves." He strained against his ropes. They cut into his hands. From her spot on the floor, Neta saw the stake rattling in the ground. It inched upward. She couldn't be sure if it was real or just the concussion.

A short figure cast a long shadow from between

a pair of pillars. The room had stopped circling her enough for Neta to recognize her. Agda. Her face was painted with a thick smattering of grey mud, three parallel lines across either side, intersecting with a thicker line down the middle separating her tiny black eyes. No, not Agda. Another Bethian.

"Nkokon. Hello devils," the Bethian said, her gravel voice harsher than Agda's. "A storm is coming. It is time to go." She approached the Judge, yelling his profanity-laden protests. In her hand, she revealed a knife. A bone polished until it possessed a reflective sheen. She delivered a hard punch to the Judge's stomach with the handle.

"We know the secrets of your shapes," said the gravelly voice, "all of your stories.

"Nkokon. What you see around you, in this canyon," the Bethian continued, "this is all there is. Nothing exists beyond. You devils came, in your new shapes, with a lie on your tongue: that there was an endless canyon beyond Intiloch. The other tribes may have believed, but not the Tamal. The Tamal can see through your disguises for what you are.

"Nkokon—" he repeated.

"What does that mean? Why do you keep saying that?" the Judge demanded.

"It's their name," Neta said from the ground, "they identify themselves every time they start a new thought. A hold out from the native tongue."

"This is insane," the Judge protested. Two more Bethians appeared between pillars whispering in hums and clicks.

"Another colony went missing a few months ago,

we think the Tamal took them. They must have learned our language from the prisoners," Neta whispered.

"This life is only the soil where our bodies are planted," the priest continued, "allowing our spirits to ripen, to be cultivated and harvested. To nourish the Old Shapes, the evil things that lay waiting on the other side. We are little more than grass to the Old Shapes, purposely sown, to be plucked from the stalk in our prime.

"That was before the great moon, Intiloch, came and pushed them back. We cannot see the Old Shapes, though they are still among us. They hide over the great walls, daring to descend in the storms of sand," the Bethian called loudly, warning her evil gods. An approving grunt came from the newcomers, and from outside the temple, a small crowd of maybe a dozen voices had gathered that had been eerily still and silent before. "And we see you for what you are."

"What is that?" Neta asked. She covered her eyes as a sharp wind blew black sand into her face.

"We've seen what you did to our brothers," the Bethian said to the Judge. Neta guessed it was a leader or priest, probably both. They turned their attention toward her. "And we know what you will do to us and our canyon. You are the children of the Old Shapes. Their servants who would plow the fields, all at once, in hopes of giving your masters a mighty feast."

The Bethian lifted her small hands to their goddess, the dark clouds finding their place at her side. "Intiloch protects us. She lets us over-ripen. To spoil into old age when her kin will no longer have a taste for our souls. She is one of them, herself an Old Shape, from the other side of the darkness. She came to scare away her wicked brethren, who would fill their stomachs. Each morning she rises over the world to keep the hordes at bay, driving them back once more. Her battle is exhausting. Her journey here was a hard one. She needs our help to continue.

"She is dying. With every storm, she gasps and cries to us for nourishment. So she can fight on. That has been the purpose of this tribe for millennia, since our creation, to ensure that Intiloch has been fed. We found her food." The priest stared deep into Neta's eyes. "Because of your people, so many of mine have made the sacrifice to provide for her survival. We did this so all of the people of the canyon will be free from the stomachs of the Old Shapes. So they could leave this world in their old age when they would have a sour taste. They would be discarded by the monsters and free to travel to what lies even further beyond them."

"This is nonsense," growled the Judge, straining against his ropes.

"That must be why the city is so empty," Neta whispered to him, "they've killed so many of their own as sacrifices to the moon."

The priest turned her attention back to the Judge. A dozen Bethians crowded the space between the pillars. Slowly, they moved toward the center of the temple. "Nkokon. the Old Shapes sent you here. To build your cities and lure the other tribes to the protection of your machines. No longer able to sustain the demands, we plucked ourselves all but bare. We have dried up. We are in famine." Standing over the Judge, the priest lifted the knife over her head. "They made a mistake in sending you here. Intiloch doesn't care where her meal comes from, as long as she is fed."

The Judge pushed forward, meeting the coarse blade with the soft meat of his shoulder. It happened quickly but felt like time extended. The knife moved through his skin, each imperfection tearing inward, widening the hole. Neta could not describe the sound he released as a scream. It was a guttural howl, originating in a place outside of reality, born of metaphysical rage and murderous desires. The stake snapped easily as if he could have done it earlier if he had wanted.

Even with one arm crippled from the knife in his shoulder, the Judge's power was terrifying. He grabbed and lifted Nkokon the Priest over his head with a single, thin working arm, and crushed him against a stone pillar. The Bethians rushed from the borders of the temple and threw their tiny bodies at the beast. Their strength lay in numbers, but Neta could only watch as he tore them apart. Breaking limbs and ripping leathery exoskeletons. Gritty cries poured from little mouths. The moon hung high in the sky above, watching it all, doing nothing to protect her disciples.

"Nkokon. Intiloch still hungers," the priest called, his body broken against a pillar. The Judge released another howl, a sound only their most primal ancestors would understand.

He could kill them all, Neta knew with a horrifying realization. He hadn't been lying when he said that he would. She understood why terraforming was an appealing business to the man. Like Rob had told them, 'It would strip away all of what makes this planet unique. An entire ecosystem wiped out from the bottom-up.' He would do all of it with his bare hands if he had the time. She believed he was honest about doing the same to her and the colony. A one-man swarm of evil and hatred released upon the land. Seeing as he was busy tearing through their captors, Neta decided it was a good time to start running.

What she decided and what she was capable of, however, were very different. Barely able to drag herself to her feet, Neta stumbled to the barrier of stone pillars. The world twisted sideways, as she braced against a column. Beyond the village, the familiar bare desert of black sand and a sky blotted out of view by even blacker clouds. The approaching maelstrom wasn't like the storms that Neta grew up with. Angry smears of ink filled the sky, heavy downpours of rain, and exhilarating flashes of light. This was a phantasm that reached from the ground to the sky, filled with sand.

Neta stopped at the long staircase, built for smaller feet than her own. She resolved herself to take several steps at once, fighting her dizziness, pushing against the wind and grains of sand stinging her face. Her world continued to spin, causing her to trip over her own feet with every other stride. She moved forward, keeping an eye on the wall approaching in the distance.

The entrance of the longhouse found Neta, again

Exogeny

ready to vomit. She regretted having nothing to give it. Through the empty doorway, she heard a familiar voice, "Look, Mommy, first steps." She peeked around the corner. A lone Bethian waited in the middle of the room, craning its head side-to-side. It had not seen or heard her. In its small fingers, it held her wristband. The guard twisted a small dial, pulling up the last image she had viewed. The video of the olive-skinned child stumbling towards the camera repeated. "Look, Mommy, first steps," the man repeated off-camera.

From outside the hut, a cheer rose from the direction of the pyramid, quickly deafened by the growing winds. The guard quickly turned toward the sound. Something had it on edge. Neta waited patiently for it to return its attention to the device, twisting it over its hands. When the moment was perfect, Neta called out as loudly as she could muster, "Flashlight, on!"

The beam of light pointed directly into the face of her would-be captor. The guard fell back against a wall, grasping at its small sensitive eyes with stubby hands. It yelped with a pain Neta almost sympathized with. She rushed forward anyway. If she was going to be on the attack, now was the time. She lifted her arms above her head, ready to bring them down hard.

"Neta, stop, I'm here to rescue you!" the creature said, struggling to cover her eyes with a pair of goggles that Neta hadn't seen in its hands.

"Agda?" Neta asked. "Oh, thank god." The dash across the room allowed her stomach to find one last ounce of liquid. She fell to the floor and again vomited hot bile. She spat out what little saliva she could muster to clear the taste from her mouth.

"I'm so sorry," she said, pulling herself forward to her small friend. "How did you get here?"

"Erickson left me a message before you left, telling me what you two were planning." Agda steadied herself, blinking hard. "I followed his map and saw the smoke of the burnt-out RV, then followed the tracks here."

The bottom fell out of Neta's stomach.

"Do you know where they are holding him?" Agda asked. Neta could tell by the look on her face that Agda had already guessed when she found he wasn't in the hut.

"Agda, he didn't..." Neta began but couldn't finish the sentence. So much had happened. She had done so much in a short amount of time. They didn't look at each other. Hoarse moans pulled from Agda's throat.

The call came closer than before: "Nkokon. Intiloch still hungers."

"I'm sorry," Neta said, "but we need to get out of here. What's the plan?"

"I don't have a plan," Agda said, lost in her sadness. "I was just searching for him. I wasn't expecting a jailbreak."

A chorus of scratchy voices all sounded at the same time, declaring themselves all separately, coming together to echo the distinctive chant "Intiloch still hungers" through the intensifying winds.

"Alright. We can make this work." Neta said,

crouching over the pile of equipment against the reed woven wall. "Bag and helmet," she told herself, remembering the important items in the room. "Hold these," she said to Agda, piling the gear in her open arms. Neta picked up the rifle in the pile of equipment. Not wanting to make the same mistake twice, she fumbled with a switch on the side of the blaster and changed the setting to spread.

Neta pointed the rifle at the back wall.

Gravelly cries sounded from just outside the doorway as she took the helmet from Agda. Neta led her through the hole, pushing through loose grass that refused to be fully removed. On the other side she stopped as her foot touched the sand. Just past the center of the sky, within the silent vacuum of space, Intiloch hung in pieces. A molten flare ejected in slow motion from the moon's core, pulling darkening crust into the tight orbit.

"Agda?" Neta asked, "what's that?"

"Oh, yeah, that happens occasionally."

Agda grabbed her and pulled her forward. Hand in hand they ran, the cries of the Tamal piercing over the chaos that surrounded them. Above them light erupted in long quick slashes of fire as cooled expulsions from the broken moon burned like phosphorus in the atmosphere. Not to be outdone, the approaching sandstorm raced like a banshee to consume them, eventually drowning out the meteor shower. It was only a short distance before they were lost in the swirling black winds.

She couldn't breathe. Every time she opened her

mouth, it filled with sand. She didn't dare to stop moving for fear of being buried. She pushed onward, unable to see in the dark of the storm, the light of the decaying moon blotted out. The flashlight only illuminated the sand stinging her face. In front of her, she could see Agda leading the way, but nothing beyond. Neta was unsure which direction they headed. Their hands clasped tightly together. She feared letting go of her friend even for a second, knowing that doing so meant losing each other.

As they moved against the gale, she placed the Judge's helmet over her head. It was bigger than hers, but the clasps aligned to the chest plate of her jumpsuit. A built-in ventilator activated as she snapped the latches closed. She had been without fresh air for too long. She didn't know yet what damage had been done, but she was positive that her elbow, like her wrist, had become harder to move.

Hours passed of blind wandering when suddenly Agda tugged against her arm. Neta looked down, seeing Agda place a short finger over her lipless mouth. Neta flicked off her flashlight and searched through the storm for any movement. Standing still, she felt a rhythmic uneasiness in the shifting sands. Through the grains pelting her helmet and the storm raging around them, she saw another set of lights cutting through the dark, the distinctive octagonal high beams of the ShuttleCrawler. The Judge had survived, assuming a man like that was capable of dying. Neta wondered if perhaps he could sustain himself forever on violence and hatred. Perhaps the Tamal were right, that he had been sent by their pantheon of evil gods. There was something unnatural about his strength and the way he moved. He had managed to make his way back to his vehicle far quicker than she would have thought possible.

Slowly she crouched down, making herself as small as possible. The lights lifted then turned as the vehicle trudged away into the distance, moving its mechanical legs through the desert. He may not have seen them, she thought, or he was simply leaving them to the storm.

In the last light of the retreating crawler, Neta saw a silhouette. Agda saw it too. It was small, another Bethian, most likely from the Tamal village. Neta freed her hand from Agda's grip and unslung the rifle from around her shoulders. Agda grabbed her around the waist, not wanting to get left behind. She pressed the stock tight into her shoulder. She had it, she wasn't the best shot in the universe or even on this planet, but she had it. She knew it.

The trigger hardly budged, grinding against the sand that had infiltrated every part of its mechanics. It wouldn't fire. She squeezed harder. Something inside gave way and released with a small cracking sound. The trigger moved freely, separate from the rest of the gun's innards, flopping freely forward and backward.

The creature turned towards them in the black blizzard of sand. Multiple shadows emerged from the darkness getting closer. Agda pulled at Neta, still fumbling with the broken trigger.

"This way," she mouthed. They ran for long minutes, Neta following Agda's lead.

Neta didn't notice they had entered the mouth of a cave until they were several meters past the threshold, the wind dying down, the air clearing, and her round helmet no longer assaulted with grains of sand.

"What is this?" Neta asked.

"Tunnels under the Arid Mountains. The first humans dug them."

They kept their pace, knowing the pursuers were close behind. Neta ducked behind a set of large black-grey boulders far enough back that the little light permeating the entrance of the cave had all but extinguished. Every surface—floor, wall, and ceiling—was wet with condensation and stained with minerals built up from long abandonment. Neta held Agda close to her chest, staying as silent as possible. She turned off the filter built into the helmet, reducing the hum it produced to silence. Releasing the clasps that held it airtight to her suit would create too much noise, she knew. She turned her head to peek around the side of their hideout, the glass of her helmet starting to fog with the condensation from her breath.

Through the moisture, she could see the priest, Nkokon, face paint smeared and bone-knife in hand. He limped into the cave cautiously. Behind, half a dozen of the tribesmen followed, all injured in some way. They wandered through the cave, searching the crevices and behind outcroppings. One Bethian, a strip of leathery hide missing from its chest revealing the white meat underneath, came close to their boulder. Neta held her breath. The oxygen in the helmet was depleting quickly. What little air was left would

Exogeny

not last. The creature paused. It stopped, neglecting to look behind the rock, and walked back to the entrance where the others stood in a circle around their leader.

"Grl. Intiloch still hungers." said the creature with the hole in its chest as it joined the circle.

Nkokon firmly repeated the call. And again, the followers echoed in unison.

The priest placed the handle of the bone knife into the hand of the Bethian who had identified themselves as Grl. Together, both of their hands on the knife, Nkokon and Grl, pushed the blade between the plates of Nkokon's thorax with a quick hard motion. Neta turned away, her head spinning, but she heard the gruff cry as the air pushed out from the priest's lungs combined with the thumping from the frantic kicking of his legs against the stone floor. The noises echoed through the tunnel, found a wall, then made their return. Soon the death groans came to an end. Slowly the reverberations died too. Neta and Agda sat silently, the helmet filling with carbon dioxide. As she thought only of sleeping, Neta heard the natives rustling near the entrance, dragging their leader with them against the floor.

"They're gone," Agda said after a moment, she reached up and activated the filter of Neta's helmet.

Neta took deep, desperate breaths of clean, oxygenated air. Her senses returning, she slid down the side of the boulder, putting her helmeted head between her legs.

"We need to go before they come back," Agda said, stepping around the boulder, facing the entrance of the cave.

"Not that way," Neta said, looking up, "we don't know how many came. They may be waiting outside."

"We go deeper?" Agda asked, "we don't even know if it leads anywhere."

Neta looked at the cave. As it went further back, the tunnel became less bumpy, smoother, and polished. She ran her hand along the wall at her side, flicking on the flashlight at her wrist. The tunnel was circular, almost perfectly, with corkscrew waves of rock jutting slightly out toward them.

"You said the survey team dug this?" she asked.

"Yes, they dug this cave and left."

Neta pulled herself to her feet and tapped a button on her wrist. A map flickered to life on her screen. "If the survey team dug these for mineral samples..." she trailed off as the image zoomed in on the mountain range they couldn't see through the sandstorm. A series of blue tunnels, cutting through one end of the mountain, coming out another. "We have a map of it."

They trekked the long tunnel drilled through the black-grey stone of the mountain range.

"I didn't know you had a child," Agda said, breaking the silence.

"I do," Neta said, shining the light deeper into the tunnel.

"What are you doing here?"

"We needed the money," she lied, "and this job paid too well to pass up."

"It must be hard being so far away for so—"

"I don't want to talk about it," Neta cut her off,

"I'm very good at not talking about it."

"Why not?"

"You're not supposed to talk about it. What happened is hard to admit to and hard to hear. It makes other people uncomfortable."

Agda pondered quietly for a minute. "That is a complication. What is the point of such detailed languages if you're not able to express how you are feeling?"

"She's just better off this way, her father can handle it himself." Neta picked up her pace a little, putting some distance between herself and Agda, whose short legs couldn't make the stride. "They need me here, where I can—could—send money back. More than they needed me there."

"It seems to me that you need them, though," Agda said, calling ahead.

Neta stopped at the edge of a large cavern. On the opposite end, the tunnel continued. Dead in the center, another tunnel of equal size led straight down. Neta looked at the map as Agda caught up. "It'll be night soon," Neta said, "we should rest here."

"Where does that go?" Agda asked, pointing to the hole.

"Nowhere we want to," Neta said. In the map, it led straight down for kilometers, where it branched off into a web of further downward tunnels. "It's where the Cornflower Company found the minerals they were looking for."

They sat silent against the damp wall, the cold sinking through Neta's suit.

"What happened to him?" Agda asked finally,

finding the words harder to form.

"Erickson? Are you sure you want to know?"

"Yes."

Neta told her of everything that had occurred while holding her small friend in the darkness of the cavern. Finding Eddy, the shot that killed Erickson, how his body had burned with the ShuttleCrawler, and of her experience with the Tamal. Agda wailed a long sharp note, like the one she had let out in the commissary. That cry had been from fear and surprise. This was one of sorrow. There was wetness and sustaining vibration to the sound, originating deep from within her thorax heaving under Neta's arms. Neta did her best to comfort, trying to atone for her role, stroking the shell on Agda's back. They held each other for what felt like hours until finally, outside the labyrinth of tunnels, Intiloch set behind the canyon walls. She watched as Agda fought hard against the coming sleep, not wanting her grief to slip away. If she slept, she wouldn't hurt, and that would be a betrayal. Eventually, though—as it always does—biology won.

Alone with only the light from her wristband, dimmer in the vast openness of the chamber, Neta sat in silence. It would be hours before they would be able to continue. Unwilling to deal with her thoughts, Neta fumbled with the rifle, flipping the useless trigger back and forth. She pulled down on the side, removing a panel that gave her access to the blaster's inner workings, learning quickly she had no actual idea of what she was doing. Not only was she unable to mend the long metal rod snapped in half,

Exogeny

but she also wasn't able to identify its actual purpose. The scattered pieces refused to return to anything resembling their original configuration.

Slowly a dull, repetitive clicking echoed through the chamber. It was impossible to identify its origin in front, behind, or below. She looked at the assorted pieces on the ground in front of her. Carefully, Neta picked up the core, a battery the size of her fist. She turned it over, making sure there were no punctures or reason for it to be the source of the sound.

"It's probably just water. It's all down there somewhere," she said to Agda, sleeping silently by her side.

She heard it again, small rocks being moved and falling. Quickly, Neta pushed the rifle's ruined innards away on the stone floor. All except its core, fitting it snuggly in her pocket.

"Agda," Neta whispered, fruitlessly shaking her friend, knowing full well that nothing would wake her until the moon rose. Could it be the Tamal returned? Or something worse? No one knew what would be found in Beth's underground channels of water. If the Cornflower Mining Corporation couldn't have been trusted to properly keep their accounting team from embezzling employee pensions, how could they be trusted to perform biodiversity surveys? Or was it nothing at all, just the natural echoes of condensation dripping to her exhausted and traumatized ears?

Neta began pulling Agda face-first across the floor, straining to drag her more than just a few meters. She looked around as the echoes grew louder. Time to run, she thought, pushing away the stray idea to leave

Agda behind. She grabbed her from under the armpits and heaved the small, round frame up against the cavern wall. Neta bent down low onto her knees and let her sleeping friend fall forward onto her shoulders. Hunched over and her helmet pushed forward, she circled the chasm, careful to keep her distance.

She followed the directions of her wristband through a series of interweaving tunnels, quickening her hobbled pace. If still accurate, they would exit on the opposite side of the mountain range from the Tamal tribe. She felt Agda stir on her aching shoulders.

"Neta..." Agda said sleepily, her involuntary slumber over.

"Almost there." She called over her shoulder.

"I hear something."

Agda's long ears perked up. They hadn't lost it in the maze of tunnels as Neta had hoped. The sound followed closely behind them, a rhythmic scraping, like too-many limbs skittering against rocks.

The light of the outside world beamed its dim red light from a hole in front of them. Neta pushed herself harder, Agda jostling around on her back. They dove out the opening, the ground disappearing from below their feet. Together they tumbled down a sharp incline of loose sand, rolling end over end.

Neta looked up to their exit. A wet, bulbous shape filled the mouth of the cave. A small head made entirely of two symmetrical jaws that seemed to open and close separate from each other protruding from the end of the slug-like body. A simple, shapeless ball, lacking all features except for an orifice filled with large, yellowed teeth that encircled a series of deep tear-drop-shaped holes, the sensory functions of which Neta was positive she wouldn't understand.

It did not dare to follow them. From the appearance of its translucent skin—pulled tight over its bloated body, pink organs visible beneath—it had not felt the touch of the world outside the tunnel in its life. A primordial remnant of the cold, lonely planet that had existed before Intiloch had arrived, pushed underground by the loss of complete darkness. An eyeless and faceless terror that would have found even the barren world above the canyon unbearable. To it, the warmth of the air and moon was the greater monster.

"What is it?" Neta asked, climbing to her feet as quickly as she could, ready to run.

"An Old Shape," Agda said, confused by her own words.

All of the Tamal priest's rants of strange mythology, those stories don't just emerge from a vacuum, Neta thought. This swollen creature was the missing link on which those myths were based.

The Old Shape snapped angrily at the air around its misshapen jaw, trying to grab ahold of the formless enemy that stabbed at it with hot knives. Hundreds—maybe thousands—of small arms, like the swimmerets attached to the underside of a crustacean, coiled down the swollen behemoth's body in thin paired lines, converging and ending around the enraged head. The miniature limbs began fanning back and forth, creating the illusion of their forked black claws spiraling as they slowly propelled the body back into the comforting darkness of the cave.

Once the Old Shape had disappeared completely, Neta looked around. They stood at the entrance of a dead orchard, thin trees close to a dozen meters tall, with long branches reaching out toward the sky. There were dozens of them expanding further and further back, covered in the same smooth bark that ran up Neta's arm, only grey, dried, and twisted. Thick white flakes rained down around them, blanketing the ground and resting on their shoulders.

"Snow?" Neta asked.

"I don't think it snows here," Agda said, "I've never seen it, at least."

Neta held out her hand and caught a falling flake. It sat still in her palm, not melting or changing. No glittering crystals made up its structure. She poked it with a gentle finger. It crumbled into a powder at her slight touch.

"Ash," said Neta. She looked to the sky, the broken moon was lost behind thick white clouds, its light diffusing over the valley. She reached up to touch the surface of the closest branch. Lifeless twigs broke easily.

"Have you ever seen anything like this?" Neta asked. Agda shook her head no. They moved forward through the forest, looking up to the canopy. She opened the image of their map. She needed a bearing of their location. It didn't make sense. They were at Colony1. Right outside the barracks. Neta closed the map and moved her arm. For the first time since they exited the cave, she looked at the ground, to the moss field that the tree sprouted from.

Around the base of each tree, a beaten and battered light-blue jumpsuit, glass helmets, and filters were strewn along the ground.

"Cornflower gear," Neta said, comparing it to her patchwork jumpsuit. "Provided to all their employees." There were no signs of bodies, no remains left in the deflated suits. The infection had taken every bit and eaten it away, using every morsel of skin, bone, and hair. Now, the plant had run out of food, shriveled and died.

The ground was littered with sharp burnt shrapnel that had once been the plastic squares of dome walls. Beyond the trees, a plume of smoke rose. The colony's generator system had blown, sending shards of plastic ripping through the rest of the domes and inhabitants.

"The sandstorm," Neta said. "The one that took down our communications center. It tore right through Colony1 while they slept."

Slowly they walked through the orchard of Neta's peers. She had known some of them. Talked to them on the radio. A few had even taken a trip to Colony2 to trade resources and share information. A brief movement caught their eyes. A shape lumbering through the trees, draped in the familiar blue suit. The lone colonist turned and disappeared into the ruins of the domes.

"Wait here," Neta said, leaving Agda behind. She carefully made her way forward. There was little left of the colony other than burnt foundations, melted plastic walls, and destroyed electronics. No sign of the survivor. Within the remnants, more trees sprouted, marking the graves where colonists had fallen. Quietly she came around a corner, unsure she wanted to find anything there. But there it was, shallow empty sockets staring directly into her. His helmet was shattered, sharp pieces of glass protruded from the remaining collar. The face before her was wooden, replaced entirely with the virus. Wide strips of curling bark pulled away from the skin and fell lightly to the ground. The nose and ears long ago were eaten away and closed. Only the mouth remained, trapped wide open in a Munchian shriek. Fungal offshoots pulled out of the center of the forehead, reaching heavenward in discipleship of Intiloch. A wayward hand blindly pushed against her shoulder. Neta fell backward and screamed. Her cries echoed within her glass helmet. The man's arms flew about him wildly searching the air for the quickly forgotten touch of another person.

Neta backed away as the survivor lost balance in its enthusiasm. He tripped blindly in front of her, a cloud of ashy dust in his wake. Loudly his lungs gargled for a gasp of air. Neta pulled herself to him and pushed her hands underneath him, heaving to roll him onto his back. His wheezing stopped as the Bark squeezed the last of his windpipe shut. His hand fished through the air with a panic. Neta did the only thing she was sure she could, she grabbed his hand in her own and held it. His body shook, fighting and convulsing. Neta tightened her grip and squeezed it several times, hoping to convey a message, though she wasn't sure what exactly it was she was trying to say. After a minute the shaking stopped, and the hand relaxed in her grip. Neta held on a little longer, just in case there was any part of the man left, so he wouldn't be alone if there was. Gently she placed his hand onto his chest and left him to join his comrades.

"What happened?" Agda asked as Neta returned to her in the orchard.

"Nothing. I thought I saw something, but I was wrong."

Only a single structure of Colony1 remained unscathed—with the exception of a tear along the sidewall—the sturdier medical dome, constructed of stronger materials than the rest of the colony. Neta approached the exterior entrance. At her feet, she counted a series of deep circular indentations recently left in the ash and sand by a series of eight mechanical legs.

In the middle of the medical dome stood another aspen-like tree, shorter than the ones outside. Its growth had been cramped by the limited height available within, but it compensated with a thick, flaking bulb at the base. A white lab coat crushed under the weight of the roots. Whatever piece of shrapnel tore its way through the dome's wall had found the colony's doctor. While Neta searched the cabinets and drawers, Agda patched the hole with a repair kit found in the building's emergency equipment in case of minor damage. The sheet of tarp almost didn't cover the tear to the plastic walling, needing to adjust the angle to allow the corners to just barely cover the gash. She sprayed a polymer over the patch to solidify it in place, sealing them inside. After a few minutes, the air filters cleansed the room. Neta removed the Judge's stolen helmet.

"Found it!" she declared. She held up a small vial, clear liquid sloshed around inside, the word 'Capozole' written in bold letters on the side.

"That's it, that's what all this was about?"

"That's right."

Neta unzipped her jumpsuit. Stiffly, she pulled out her arm. The Bark had spread across her fingers, up past the elbow. More concerning were small buds cropping up, little knobs protruding outward. She placed the vial in an auto-injector, a short white tube hiding a hypodermic needle, able to assess the correct dosage for a patient just by touching the tip of the hollowed end to the skin. She pressed the injector to her bicep. A series of lights activated as the sensors analyzed her condition.

"Do you see that?" Agda said, crouching down at the base of the tree that had once been the doctor.

Neta kneeled beside her, removing the injector. The lights deactivated. The whirring of small, computerized motors came to a halt. She peeled a bright blue glob of chewing gum from a gap in the smooth wooden protrusion at the base of the tree.

"Yeah, the Judge was here," she said.

"The tourist?"

"It's the same gum that he had in the commissary. The stuff he put on Lolo's forehead." She flicked it to the ground. "It's still sticky. He wasn't here long ago. Last night probably."

"That's not what I was looking at, though," Agda said. Her stubby fingers ran over the bark where the gum had been removed. She outlined the curves of a familiar shape, flattened and dulled from the infection eating away all signs of humanity. The doctor's body was still discernible, even if just, within the mass of plant-like matter, not like the others they had seen. Maybe the medical dome's air filters slowed the speed that the corpse was engulfed, Neta wondered.

"She's holding something," Agda said.

Neta saw it, a reflection of light on glass from between the wooden arms, the branches wrapped around a glass globe, the body folded over it protectively. The vertebrae of the spine could easily have been mistaken for knots in the wood. She turned the flashlight on, shining the light through, outlining a dark shape fidgeting within. She grabbed the arms to release them from their dead grip, straining for her infected hand to grasp close.

"Don't think about it," Neta said, mostly to herself, commanding her brain to forget the reflection of her advancing future. The Bark flexed slightly in her grip and snapped, the softwood dead and dusty. It had been easier than she expected or wanted it to be. She fell backward into Agda, throwing the broken arms away from herself out of instinctual disgust.

"It's a helmet," Agda said, confirming what Neta had already guessed. Inside the clear glass, she could see a small grey blanket wrapped like a cocoon.

"How do we get it out?" she asked. The late doctor's head, smoothed and deflated, still draped over the helmet, holding it firmly in place.

Neta sighed as she grabbed beneath the wooden growth. She looked down. It was a mistake. She could distinguish the mouth, and nose, and worst of all the eyes, not quite erased from the face she held in her hands.

"Goddamnit," she muttered. She looked away and pulled up quickly. It snapped easily, fracturing unevenly midway through the neck. It clattered on the ground. She didn't see where, refusing to look. Neta walked away to collect herself.

Agda pulled the helmet from the hollow cavity it had left in the doctor's body. The tips of her fingers slipped on the smooth surface. There was a heaviness to it that she wasn't expecting. She pointed the makeshift lid towards Neta, taped together scraps of a jumpsuit forming an improvised cap along with the neck seal. Neta undid the clasps and reached inside. The size and weight of the object within the helmet were too familiar for her as she lifted it out of the helmet.

She removed the blanket to reveal what she already expected: a baby, newly born, soft, and pink-skinned. It was warm and heavy in her arms, squirming in its sleep. Neta put her hand on its chest, feeling it move up and down with each breath. An anxious habit she could never break from doing with her child.

"The doctor must have been holding him during the storm," Neta said.

"Oh no," Agda said. Neta hadn't seen it. Once she had, she wasn't sure how she could have missed it. The side of the child's neck was smooth green-brown. Hard to the touch. The infection had spread, creeping up onto a chubby cheek. Neta pulled back the blanket.

"How bad?" Agda asked.

"Really bad. All the way down the side. To his thigh."

Neta handed the baby to Agda's small open arms. A little cry came from his little mouth. She held him close to her thorax, instinctually shushing and rocking him. Neta picked up the auto-injector from the table. She examined it closely. Remembering what she had done to get it, she had killed and almost been killed. She looked over at her companion. Agda held the baby like it was her own, never looking away and giving it a small kiss on the forehead with a long snout-like mouth. He grunted quietly in his sleep. She would never let harm come to the child. It had no one else who would look at it with the same shine to her eyes.

"Here," Neta said, stepping towards them.

"Are you sure?"

"He needs it more than I do."

Agda shifted the sleeping baby in her arms, exposing the little shoulder that was still made of skin. Neta placed the auto-injector in position. The lights activated one-by-one around the tip of the tube. The glow switched to green, telling them that everything was ready. She pressed a small button on the side of the tube. The vial of liquid emptied. The child woke immediately, crying in a fury. Agda paced the room, cradling it in her small arms, making the same clicking noises Neta had heard other Bethians make to their young.

On the floor, Neta saw the bright-blue chewing gum staring back at her. The Judge had been right here. He would have seen between the branches. He had placed the gum on the glass of the helmet. He had known the baby was there. It would have been impossible to miss.

With the pieces of Intiloch low in the canyon's morning sky, Neta and Agda and the baby secured in its helmet filled their hydration packs and took what comforts they could scavenge from the dome. They hiked across the black sands, keeping the Stacks far away in the distance. To pass the time, they pointed to waves of magma on the moon's surface, naming shapes that formed to fill the void left by the fracture. When they grew tired of their game, Neta insisted Agda tell her the story of the Alkayon, an ancient tower so impossibly tall its spire would scrape the moon.

The day came to an end as they reached the border where the desert met the rocky highlands. Neta pitched the tent from the Judge's stolen supply pack on the first patch of soft moss where the sand had begun to recede. Agda fell asleep through a mixture of joy for the child cradled in her arms and grieving sobs. The loss of Erickson finally caught up with her after the distraction of the long hike.

"He pursued me, you know," Agda told her as she began drifting off. "It took me a long time to realize what he was doing. Flirting and courting me like that. It's not how my people did things. But he could always pick me out of a crowd. No other human had been able to tell me apart from all the others. He could do it, though."

Neta pulled a packet of formula they had found in the supply cabinets from the pack. Mixing the powder was more difficult than it should have been. Her hand no longer followed her commands, frozen in an arthritic grip. She removed her glove, shaking loose the final four fingernails onto the floor. The humanity in her hand was gone. Though the shape of it was the same, nothing else remained but the woody Bark.

"Shit," she screamed in frustration. The baby followed her lead, wailing loudly at her outburst.

"Sorry," Neta apologized half-heartedly, "not you. You're a good baby."

She lifted him from Agda's sleeping arms. He took the bottle quickly and easily. She held him close, remembering the way it felt when things were good, "but you're not mine." She placed the child in the blanket-lined helmet he had used for a crib between her and Agda.

Halfway through the sleepless night, her wristband gave three quick chirps. Colony2 had been able to reconfigure the servers she had sabotaged. Messages flooded into the dashboard, too many to read on such a small screen. She pressed down on one of the small buttons, switching over to the map. An orange dot displayed that had not been there before, pulsing against the cartography. It was the ShuttleCrawler.

"I guess you're right, Agda. I probably need to see my baby," she told her sleeping companions.

Neta left before they awoke, taking only her uncharged blaster and the power core of the discarded rifle. The two pieces, being what the other lacked, proved incompatible with the other. Like Erickson had before, she left a note. She told her friend to take the boy to Dr. Canalis. Then, as soon as possible, use the credits Erickson had saved to get herself and the child off of the planet to somewhere capable of helping him. Colony2 was only a day's walk away, and Agda was sturdy. She could handle it with the added load.

Neta followed the frontier toward the unmoving dot.

The Judge was lost and had been since he escaped the leather-skinned aliens into the sandstorm. He never noticed when the communications network activated, so lacking was his faith in the colonists to get a radio tower working. He lay on the sloped hood of the SRV, parked at the crest of a dune overlooking a ragged-edged cliffside that dropped into the bottom of a deep valley. He counted the stars he would destroy as they slowly blinked out of the sky, lost in the burgeoning morning light.

"Yes, just like that," he said, smiling his wicked smile, as the universe extinguished from view. His attention shifted to movement below him, a blue-jumpsuit walking along the edge, round bubble helmet bouncing along at a quick pace. His helmet.

"Finally," he said. The colonist saw him and started walking in his direction. He laid his head back against the warm glass windshield as he waited for her to trudge up the loose sands of the dune.

She stopped, several meters away, next to the driver's door. He didn't have to look to know she was silently staring at him. "Took long enough," he said without opening his eyes, "I've been searching for your colony for a few days now."

"I'll give you a map, but I need something from you first," Neta said.

"Seems to me like you already have plenty that doesn't belong to you," he said, "I'll be needing that helmet back, by the way."

"We can talk about who keeps what later." She was bolder than she had been when they first met in the commissary. She stood taller and straight. She was more confident. Too confident for his liking.

"You know the rules. I can't give you any supplies. Things get messy if I do."

"Then you're not giving me anything. I'm taking it."

He heard the familiar click of a holster unfastening. It was enough for him to open his eyes. Her blaster was already drawn.

"Still asking about your antifungal?"

"I'm not asking anymore," she told him.

"You know, I made my decision about this planet days ago when that little kitchen girl didn't show us the gratitude we deserved." He sighed and slid down the hood. "I'm going to own you. And it will be worse than you could ever dream."

"You're a bastard," she told him.

"Probably," he laughed. A shadow fell between them. His smooth, undefined face twisted sharply. His pallor, now a grey-yellow, had changed in an instant. Neta felt she was seeing him properly, aged and savaged. "The paperwork is already filled out and signed. Just waiting to send. Beth and everyone on her will rot in hell. I will buy this planet. You and your ugly little friends will make me lots of money. Then I will destroy you all." Even though he stood downhill from her on the dune, his gaze still met hers at eye level.

"Terraforming is a tricky business. Accidents do happen. When you're scrubbing an atmosphere and reconfiguring it at a fundamental level, sometimes things go wrong. I can quickly strip enough ore to make up the cost and move on again." He stepped around from the front of the SRV. From his pocket, he pulled a stick of bright-blue gum and placed it in his mouth.

"Just like the baby. I know you saw him. You left your calling card there." Neta watched as he chewed.

"Nothing I could do for it. As I said, if I help, things get messy," he told her, taking slow steps up the dune towards her.

"Alright, that's close enough," she said, moving her finger to the trigger.

"I'm not going to let you use the same trick twice," he said, not missing a step.

"What trick is that?"

"Pointing a busted blaster in a stand-off, it was cute the first time, not twice though," the Judge said, stepping forward.

"You knew?" she asked. She took a small step back.

"They tend to let you know when they're working, lots of lights and sounds. Looks like your battery is dead." He grabbed the blaster out of her hand. The movement was so fast and clean, Neta only knew the gun was in his hand now.

She threw her Bark-corrupted fist like a sledgehammer, connecting her forearm with his shoulder. The patching foam he'd used to fill in the hole left by the Tamal priest's knife ripped open. Though the foam had held the wound closed, it did nothing to dull the sting. His body doubled over with the blow, every nerve screaming at once. It had been harder than he expected, like getting stabbed all over again and hit with a baseball bat at the same time, made worse by the fact that he had not foreseen the attack. It was the same arm he had crushed in his grip just days before. He'd anticipated her favoring it, not using it as a weapon.

Neta looked down at her handiwork. She thought of the Judge's attack on Mr. Lolo in the commissary and the lesson she had learned from him, to never stop hitting until it was over. She swung down again, striking the same shoulder. And again. His jumpsuit had grown wet from the open wound. He howled the same primal sound she had heard before. His eyes circled wildly until they oriented upon her, the same look of pain and berserk rage he had given the Tamal when he tore them to pieces.

She pulled back and swung her arm once more, striking it against his ear. She heard something crack but was unsure whose body the sound had come from. The Judge fell over as his world was replaced with pure white noise. He fell to the black sand at his feet. His sense of balance was lost in the final act of the beating.

When the Judge managed to orient himself, he

found he had tumbled halfway down the face of the dune. He wiped at the bloody mess of his ringing ear, finding the shape indiscernible, the cartilage battered and torn into a lumpy pulp. Above him, Neta reached for the door handle to the ShuttleCrawler. He picked himself up, his tall body hobbled over, his arm sagging and paralyzed. The blaster was freed from the holster at his waist.

"Get away from my Crawler," he growled.

Neta turned to look. He pulled the trigger immediately. The violet laser beam ripped up the incline. The high-pitched sound of energy releasing was followed by a thunderous crack. Neta felt her cheek cut open in long, thin gashes. What she hadn't felt was her wooden forearm exploding from the full impact of the shot as she used it to cover her face. The nerves, muscle, and blood vessels had been completely eaten away by the Bark that splintered into her face.

Neta stared at the stump in disbelief. She no longer had her hand or most of the forearm. Capozole wouldn't be able to fix that.

"Let's try that again," she heard the Judge crow below.

Frantically, she reached into her pocket, pulling out the battery core to Rob's rifle. Neta had seen firsthand in Eddy's SRV what happens when fuel cells rupture. She pressed a long sharp shard of her stump between a seam in the thin wrapped metal, twisting back and forth until the wooden edge found itself pried under. She jammed her shattered forearm deeper until she felt the give of puncturing the inside layer. A pillar of flame discharged, charring the

Exogeny

smooth rind of her arm and burning away the sliver that freed it from captivity.

She held the spouting flame away from her body, embers of light falling to the loose sand at her feet. The Judge had regained a modicum of his posture and steadied his blaster. Neta threw her improvised bomb as far as she could, immediately covering her head with what remained of her wooden arm, hoping to protect herself from the fireball that was sure to erupt forth.

The Judge watched with pained amusement as the battery arced and fell between them. It was a long second before the explosion, but there was no mighty detonation, only a small pop of light as Erickson had described, and a small shock wave that merely forced the Judge to take a single step further down the incline to catch his already shaky balance.

"Can we get back to it?" the Judge asked, turning his attention back to Neta.

The sand near the edge of the cliffside shifted at first, prompted by the modest jolt disturbing the delicate geological features below the ground, so slight that Neta hardly saw. The Judge didn't notice the dune behind him slowly spilling down the vertical drop. As the sand below gave way, more sand further up had no choice but to give in to gravity's demand, quickly gaining momentum.

"Alright, making it easy, I guess," the Judge said with a shrug, his attention focused on Neta taking cautious steps forward to the brow of the dune. He raised his blaster again, but the river of sand caught up to him, expanding across the edge of the cliff like the breaking of a dam. A waterfall of flowing black sand poured down to the base of the cliff below, forming a new dune. The torrent was against him. Before he could comprehend what was happening, he was pulled down and under the widening current.

Neta didn't see the Judge go over the edge. He had been buried in the deluge. She had gotten too confused and curious, too close to the edge, straining to pull her feet above the descending grains. The gravity proved too strong. She cursed herself and slipped, carried down and over the cliffside by the movement of the sand.

She landed hard on the pile below, knocking the air from her with a hard wheeze. She panicked, fighting against her abdomen, gasping for air that eventually came, but not as quickly as she wanted. She rolled over onto her side and started digging. Her hand scooped thick grains of sand to the side, her splintered stump scraping and pushing away at the hole she made. She checked her map, finding the Judge's blinking dot on the projection. She kept digging, frantic to clear the sand that only wanted to refill the hole she dug. Finally, a finger revealed itself buried underneath. It twitched, awakened by the air above. Soon she had uncovered the entire hand. It reached and grasped with hope. She let it get a hold of her wooden stump and steadied her weight as he pulled against her, attempting to free himself of the sand compressing his body. Neta was positive he would fail, no matter how strong he was. He may as well be trapped in cement. With her working hand,

Neta grabbed the clasp of his wristband and released it from his arm.

"That's all," she said, sliding her stump free from his grip. His movement became frantic. Neta pushed the sand back into the hole. The hand clawed away at the surface until it was again lost, buried completely.

The climb back to the ShuttleCrawler was long, made more difficult by Neta's loss of a hand. She pulled herself to the recreational vehicle waiting precariously on the remains of the dune. Opening the door, she was greeted by a familiar shape: a short, round, cow-like body; a glass helmet containing a small restless child pressed into the hide of her thorax. Agda rushed forward when she noticed the tattered jumpsuit, tied in a knot at the sleeve.

"What happened? Are you alright?" she asked.

Neta looked at the space her hand no longer filled. "Oh shit, where'd that go?" she said, turning to look around her, "I'm always losing that thing."

"If you're being funny, I don't get it," Agda said. Neta stepped around her and briskly walked into the back of the vehicle. Immediately, she pulled open the first aid kit on the wall and eagerly pushed the contents aside with her ruined stump, not finding what she was looking for.

"You've got to be shitting me," Neta said exhaustedly.

"Is this what you're looking for?" Agda asked behind her, holding up the small glass Capozole vial, still keeping a firm grasp on the helmet in her arms.

"Give me that," Neta said, "and take this." Neta

placed the Judge's wristband on top of the helmet and snatched the vial. Quickly, she loaded the antifungal into an auto-injector she had dropped to the floor. She placed the tube against her shoulder, just above the border of the infection. As soon as the light turned green, she pressed the button without celebration, not waiting for any new distractions. She winced at a slight prick as the needle entered her arm and the vial emptied. She sat back in relief, watching the moon set above the canyon walls.

Agda placed the makeshift crib onto an empty seat. "What are we doing with this," she asked, turning the wristband on.

"I need you to change the contract on that thing."

"Me?"

"You were Erickson's assistant. You've communicated more with these people than anyone else. You know what the paperwork is supposed to look like. Let whatever lawyers are supposed to receive this know the Judge is passing on this planet. He's already signed the documents. You just need to change the contents."

"We're lying?" Agda asked, scratching her snout in contemplation.

"We are absolutely lying about this. Do you think a company founded by people like him is going to be any better—any more altruistic—than he was? The colony can wait for the next buyer to come by. We've made it this long."

"I just wanted to make sure I understood the plan," Agda said as she began typing on a small keyboard that appeared on the screen. "What are you going to do now?"

"I'm getting off this planet," Neta told her. She drove for the rest of the day. Past dunes and cliffs and ridges. Over the moss-covered low mountains, following her map and a winding trail of reeds. Agda's attention shifted between the documents and feeding the baby, taking breaks to consider the proper legalese. The moon was approaching the eastern wall when she hit send, their home at Colony2 coming into sight. They stopped to look at the sight of the plastic domes and the tourists' StarHopper illuminated in the dimming red light.

"I've been thinking about what you asked me, when the tourists first arrived, if we Bethians were better off before the humans arrived?"

"Yeah, I remember. Have you figured out an answer?"

"I think so. Did you know that the arrival of humans saved my life?" Agda asked.

Neta shook her head.

"I was a prisoner of the Tamal. There were a lot more of them then. They went to war with my tribe. No, not war. Massacre. My tribe, we didn't have any means to defend ourselves. They invaded us. I was to be a sacrifice to Intiloch. After your people arrived, there was so much confusion I was able to escape."

"So, the answer is, yes?"

"No, my answer is no. I'll always be grateful that your people allowed me to survive and live in safety, brought me Erickson, and gave me this child. Both of whom I will always love. But I think Beth, the tribes, ruttlehorns, shrimpdeer, even the Old Shapes, everything would have been better if they were allowed to follow the natural course.

"The Tamal were never peaceful, but they weren't so fanatical before. After humans arrived, they became zealots. You were too much, too quickly. Their myths, what you told me, became more extreme. They filled in blanks with ideas they couldn't have expressed before. Pushing themselves further and further into their fears.

"If we were allowed to grow and advance at our own pace... Like what was said in the cafeteria, Beth is unique, and life grew here like it never has anywhere else. It's a shame that it couldn't be allowed to continue uninterrupted."

"Did you say shrimpdeer?" Neta asked, pushing the crawler forward to finish the last leg of their journey.

"You haven't seen the shrimpdeer yet? You would love them. They're grotesque."

Neta's gaze drifted to the sky. The mass transport they had been watching pass overhead for the last month was descending out of orbit. The large square spacecraft fired its thrusters, carefully entering the atmosphere.

"You didn't cancel the purchase?" Neta asked.

"No, I couldn't let the colonists continue suffering. They're all my friends too."

"They'll destroy everything here. Everything you said was better off without us."

Agda smiled at the baby on her lap. "For several seconds the planet, colony, and supply ship were the property of the Deering Holdings Group. However, all associated properties were immediately transferred to a nearby conservancy group. Erickson had told me about it. Colony2 will get the medicine they need, be reimbursed all due wages, then evacuated off-planet."

"You donated a planet?"

"Unfortunately, that generous gift will leave Deering without the needed capital to continue operations."

"Intergalactic business can be very tough," Neta said with a laugh.

"It's a shitshow."

Finally, Intiloch fell from view once again, her errant fracture already crashing back to her surface, a colossal stake piercing through the heart of the moon. Someday, Neta thought, in millions of years—or maybe just a few missed sacrifices—the disorder of the shifting tectonics would subside. Intiloch would cool. The Old Shapes would return from the depths and their hiding spot to the surface of the wayward planet. The way it was supposed to be.

Agda began closing her eyes. "What about you, what will you do?" Neta asked.

"I'll keep doing what I've been doing," Agda said through her emerging dreams, "I'll go with you."

Using the Judge's wristband, Neta entered the tourist's StarHopper, left abandoned on the launch pad. She strapped her friend into an empty passenger seat and secured baby Erickson at her side. Neta sat in the pilot's seat and activated the engines.

CPSIA information can be obtained
at www.ICGtesting.com
Printed in the USA
BVHW080320290922
648261BV00002B/124